NiKE

NiKE

a romance

Nicholas Flokos

A MARINER BOOK
HOUGHTON MIFFLIN COMPANY
BOSTON · NEW YORK

First Mariner Books edition 2000

Library of Congress Cataloging-in-Publication Data
Flokos, Nicholas.
Nike: a romance / Nicholas Flokos
     p.   cm.
ISBN 0-395-88396-2
ISBN 0-618-00207-3 (pbk.)
I. Title.
PS3556.L57N5 1998
813'.54 — dc21 98-11869 CIP

Printed in the United States of America

QUM 10 9 8 7 6 5 4 3 2 1

Grateful acknowledgment is made to Little, Brown and Company for
permission to reprint a line from George Seferis's poem "Santorin,"
published in *George Seferis: Poems*, translated from the Greek by Rex Warner.

Part One. Top: Photograph by Barbara Hodgson. Bottom: Map of Aegean
Sea (detail), c. 1861, private collection.

Part Two. Top: Unidentified photograph of the Louvre, n.d., private
collection. Bottom: Map of Paris (detail), c. 1900, private collection.

Part Three. Floor plan of the Louvre from *Baedeker's Paris and Its Environs*,
Leipsig: Karl Baedeker, 1881.

Part Four. Photograph of Nike (detail): Alinari/Art Resource, New York.

Needs must he sink who carries the great stones.

—GEORGE SEFERIS

PART ONE

Alistrata

Tchaglaik

Buruglaul

Karaji

Jabeili

Doanhassar

Maronia

Feredjik

Kavala

Bereketlu

Saritchaban

Gol Lagos or Karagatch

C. Fanari

Mekri

Liljakoi

Pravista

Dentheropolis

Orphano

Gulf of Contessa

Thasos

Enos

C. Paxi

G. of Istillar

C. Plati

Samothraki

Phengari M.

Samothraki I.

Athos Pena

Suvla Burun

Maltani I.

Karies

Kastri

Kurd Bau

C. Monte Santo
Athos M.
6780
C. S.t George

Imbros I.

Sedil Bahr

Hellespont

C. Drepano

Lemnos I.

Kokino

Kastro

Tenedos I.

~ 1 ~

SHE IS A SOUND TO US, the sound her name gives to a morning when the sea appears and becomes a golden mirror.

Nike. Nee-kee.

Her sea, the Aegean. Sail it, fly it, and northernmost you will see a mountain rise out of the blue. Samothrace. Island of the daughter lost, who was resurrected from centennials of sleep and abducted to Paris, to queen a museum.

The loss of the Winged Victory being an inherited loss, we Samothracians are born dispossessed. We mourn our Nike, imprisoned in the Louvre since 1863, transfixed there in noble perpetuity atop the wide Daru stairs. The Nike of Samothrace, in captivity — cut off at the larynx and armless, her wings about to close, her long chiton pressed back, audibly almost, by a wind that surged two hundred years before Christ — a sea wind, a Samothracian wind.

She survived oxidation and abrasion; she braved pirates, Turks, and Bulgars; she eluded the limekiln. Buried for centuries by an earthquake, she was unburied in fragments by a pillaging French antiquarian named Champoiseau and shanghaied to Paris aboard a French freighter.

What were we left with?

A fond despair. A covered-over hole in the ground. Archeologists call it the findspot. We call it Nike's grave, an empty grave.

Grave? say the French. Think of the spot as a navel-mark. Omphalos, you Greeks call it.

Thievery, we Greeks call it.

We have with France, you see, an unsettled score. Repatriation. Bring back our winged one, bring her home.

In a world of wrongs and cries of woe sounding up into vast spaces of cosmic night, we of Samothrace do not rage against this injustice, but we want our Nike back. Her absence is not some pleasant little folk grievance we complain to tourists about. A loss passed down from one's progenitors is a loss no less for having been suffered already, generation after generation.

Romantic loss, you might say, a mere museum piece, one marble in the great light of day. But to us her absence is like the phantom limb of an amputee. It is an absence that will not go away.

Victor Hugo said, "Without France, the world would be alone."

We of Samothrace say, Without our Nike, we are alone.

You are not alone, say tourists. Milo lost its Venus, Brooklyn its Dodgers, Britain its Princess Di.

Oh, the solace spent on us, the commiseration.

Our women are not knitters of black wool, our men do not limp compensatingly, but alone we are.

Nee-kee. Say it right, say it Greek: Nee-kee of Sam-o-thra-kee.

Tourists arrive in Nike shoes, Nike shirts, Nike caps. Nike Nike, Nike Nike ... on the travel bags they carry, on the socks and wristbands they wear. Like label locusts they come. Nike Nike, Nike Nike. We feel beset by these mispronounced letters of the English language, we feel heckled and mocked by this relentless boosterism. Nike Nike, Nike

Nike. Our Nike reducible to footwear? Her name aloft on missiles? Our Nike who stood in the open, in the ancient Sanctuary of the Great Gods, where initiates arrived from afar, from Athens and Rome, to participate in the mysteries, the rites of purification. There, standing on her flowing monumental fountain, our Nike, in her entirety, faced out on the sea from the marble prow of a ship.

Clarified now by archeological digs, the foundations of the lost sanctuary buildings are a tableau of positioned stones walked about by tourists. The Nike findspot, farthest back from the shore, looks less like a shrine abandoned than a flown coop. A low wall of weathered rocks and a simple marker, that is it. The marker identifies the findspot bilingually: Nike Fountain, ΚΡΗΝΗ ΤΗΣ ΝΙΚΗΣ. Tourists stand at these humps of stone and wonder what to feel — like mourners? or like pilgrims at the spiritual home of a hot brand of sneakers?

The runnels that fed the ancient waters to the fountain are discernible among the jasmine and the cyclamen, but rain finds speedier channels down our hillside now, down where the shovels struck.

In bad dreams we hear the shovels hired by Champoiseau. Come, dig, I pay in francs, he commands. We hear

his self-congratulatory shouts of Eureka! when a Greek digger unlocks from the earth a piece of the statue. Eureka,
shouts Champoiseau. Not *Voilà!* Even our language this cor-
sair loots.

Oh, the plunder committed in the claim Eureka!

Our Nike is not exactly the missing icon of a lost reli-
gion. She does not hold for us the sacral potency of the
Golden Fleece — but she is, in her mystical, romantic way,
ours and ours alone, our Eurydice to be brought back.

We await an Orpheus. For more than a century, we have
awaited an Orpheus. A Jason even.

What we have is Photi, courteous, sorrowful, unlucky.
His name rhymes with Quixote, but fantasies of victory do
not bedevil him. What bedevils him is defeat. Desolating
matrimonial defeats. Thrice spurned, each matrimony he
strove to enter the bonds of is evaluated in our tavernas and
coffeehouses for the scar it left on his heart. Agreed that the
second scar is twice the first and the third scar is three times
the second, we fear this exponential increase and pray that
Photi does not fall again in love.

❧ 2 ❧

*W*E ARE A SMALL ISLAND, on the map a button. Secrets are few here. It is known, village to village, that Photi's first secret flame married his second cousin, his second secret flame married his first cousin, and after his third secret flame eloped to America with his widowed father — his *patera!* — Photi became a poet. He lolled in a slingchair on the terra-cotta roof of his small white house and composed. Seen from a distance, Photi on the roof seemed like a painting there was no space for on a wall. We wished he would look less discarded, eat more, and become robuster. Knowing that the dedicatee of his poems was the memory of his mother, we envisioned the inspired rhapsodic dithyrambs and strophes. We would undervalue him, we felt, if we did not expect a masterpiece, a poem that would bring some high measure of credit to the Anthropotis name when printed in our newspaper. Though Photi was prolific, no poem of his adorned our paper. He was, he felt, a pip-squeak, not a poet, and so he jettisoned his poems — a pitiful little splash — then banished himself from the slingchair and declared himself no Cavafy, not even a Seferis. The son of our lamented Sappho and our eloped Pindaros Anthropotis — and not one poem in the columns of our paper.

Photi's belief that he is unlovable, as well as unpublishable, is perhaps his worst defeat.

Photi Anthropotis, spindly, short, and forty, has a thin face so wrung by defeat that from the back he looks to us more like himself. His neck is that of a fisherman who sat alone too long under a whaler's hat — the hat an incongruity much smiled upon because of the size of his caïque and his catches. Though at daybreak on Mondays he entered church, lit a candle, and knelt in prayer, his nets all week came back slapping slackly with small to undersized red mullet, bass, and mackerel — the pittances of a pitying Poseidon. For ten years we watched Photi's caïque come up on the curve, his hat like a stationary seabird, Photi reading a book under it, the sea under Photi, and under the sea the bottom of the world. To everything a place. Sad were we all along our shores and up and down our mountainsides when

Photi's caïque sank — it found its place on a Thursday —
the capsizing due not so much to disrepair as to Thursdays
being Thursdays and Photi being Photi.

Rescued by helicopter, Photi lost his whaler's cap to the
depths but owes his life to the pilot, his second cousin, the
one who married his first secret flame, and owes to his first
cousin, the florist who married his second secret flame, his
next line of work. For in the tavernas and coffeehouses it
was decided that Photi had been too long solitary and
needed a job that could not be done alone, such as stretcher
bearer. But no opening for stretcher bearer was foreseen
at our infirmary, so an interim job was decided on and
Photi's first cousin, smelling secondarily of the fragrance
of Photi's second secret flame, put Photi and his bicycle to
work delivering flowers.

At least, we said, Photi would know the feel of the
earth beneath his feet, and for the price of a corsage we
could have him at our door.

Indebtedness to cousins is as hefty a rock to shoulder as
defeat is, so on his nameday we drink with extra commiseration to Photi when we wish him marriage and a hundred
years of life.

Scarce is the house or maiden not visited by Photi bear-

ing flowers on his bike. Weddings, baptisms, and funerals —
there he would come, our flower, chauffeuring bouquets,
nosegays, corsages. As small as our island is, we, for the sake
of his legs and lungs, wished it were smaller. Through gales
and storms, in searing sunshine, up and down and along
our steep topography, Photi churned and huffed as though
flowers were medicine, each delivery urgent. Flowers, Photi,
and bike were a balancing act to which our narrow cobble-
stoned streets and his allergic sneeze gave his continued forward motion the aspects of a miracle. Well, if not a miracle,
then a ballet. Although we know a miracle from a difficult
two-wheeled flower delivery, we, weary of the banal mo-
tions human beings seem limited to — fishing, copulating,
and finding shade from the sun — saw Photi during his
flower-delivery years as being in rehearsal for some astonish-
ing act, some daredevil stunt that would give us reason to
boast, to the islands south, west, and east of us: Photi is of
us, he is ours.

Invited into our small white houses, Photi said he
found the cool depths of a cathedral in them, and though
we knew he had never felt the cool depths of a cathedral,
we felt it too. When time between deliveries permitted, he
downed a proffered ouzo and demonstrated to our young

how a seagull would fly if its wings were broken. Though this act of aerial adversity elicited happy laughter and sent armfuls of imaginary breezes into our rooms, we preferred to think of Photi as Photi, not as a gull with broken wings.

In the smoky councils of our coffeehouses and tavernas, it was decided that Photi could no longer suffer the allergies that worked through his nasal passages and caused him respiratory embarrassments, itching, and rashes. Photi, we agreed, must leave delivery of flowers to stronger constitutions.

Lucky for you, we told him, that just in time did your father elope to America, because now his job as guard at the sanctuary opens, and you inherit it.

So there among the ruins he walks, wearing his father's washed-out blue shirt and bent bank guard's cap. Candy wrappers, peanut shells, and soda cans he lifts and disposes of in a retired wine barrel. In the morning, he obliquely carries to the sea the occasional condom and sinks it.

"Are we," asks Photi, "a sanctuary or a bordello?"

Photi believes there exists a little Nike in every heart's niche, but this incursion of Nike sneakers, caps, and shirts, with its concomitant nihilism and loose amorality, is to him a new barbarism. He fears that we ourselves — the locals, who have Toyotas now, not donkey carts — are drifting and that the new generation, which feeds on American movies and dances to electronically amplified music, will bulldoze the sanctuary, overlay it with concrete, and gyrate on it.

Only in pictures has Photi seen our Nike — calendrical Nikes, poster Nikes, postcard and postage-stamp Nikes. The souvenir statuettes in shops annoy him, and though he is never cranky or coarse, he refuses to breathe near the cheap substitute Nike the French sent to our small museum to ease the Gallic conscience. This full-size dummy has a smell, says Photi, plaster of Paris, and constitutes a foreign occupation.

At the Nike findspot he is a host of sorts, one not easy to circumvent. Though visitors surround him, he seems to surround them, and though not tall, he is magisterial. He seems in his candle-upright way to stand for old and abandoned virtues, particularly this one: Accept no substitutes.

"By our Nike," he tells tourists, "you could measure what civilization was worth. If there was a Muse Victory, *she* would be the Muse Victory."

"Gave you the slip, did she?" twits a Brit.

"Nests don't get any emptier than that, mate," quips an Aussie.

From French tourists, even a *bonjour* comes as a slap.

Ignoring unkindnesses, Photi describes how our Nike was stolen by Champoiseau, an amateur antiquarian who visited our forefathers as a young consul from France. "Greek diggers," proclaims Photi, "turned up the Nike, and the Gaul cries Eureka! Eureka, not *Voilà!*"

Although Photi pronounces *Gaul* and *Champoiseau* without derision, we know by the set of his shoulders that the story of our Nike is far from over.

"Is it not true," asks Photi, "that a work of art ..."

Fearing a sermon, some visitors move on, but many are willing to hear more.

"... is as much a part of nature as a mountain?"

Photi looks to the snow-strewn summit of Mount Fengari (Moon Mountain, 5,400 feet). "*There* is a mountain," he proclaims, then he looks to the barren grave and sighs, "Ah! Here was a work of art."

At our small tables under the trees we do not wonder that Photi has developed a possessive passion for our Nike. We remember how it began. Photi, an adolescent, emptied of life by the death of his mother, sleeping all night in the cool summer air of the sanctuary, stretched out on a stone remnant, his hands held prayerlike, providing a pillow for his cheek. His father coming after him there, scolding him, berating him, demanding to know why, in a house with just the two of them in it, his son can find nowhere to lay his head.

And we remember Photi, a boy on his bike, his lessons over, pedaling each day in the rock-strewn sanctuary, snatching at butterflies. Around and around the ancient rocks he rode, his arms out wide as if for an embrace. "A *ptero-podilato*," he would call out. A winged bicycle. Spilled by a round marble rock that seemed to spurt from the ground, Photi and marble met head-on. Taken to the infirmary, our false-winged boy soon returned with head bandaged to the sanctuary, wrested loose the waylaying marble, and biked it home.

So self-persuaded was Photi that the marble fragment could be the missing head of the Nike, he kept it by his bed, brow to brow with a photograph of his mother. Though the marble lacked eye sockets and nose line, Photi saw a half-frown there, and through some not inexplicable extension, his mother. His father thereafter called him *petro-kefalos* (pebblehead) and *glypholept* (statue lover) and refused to allow him into the sanctuary.

Not an everyday Greek loan-word, glypholept is what they will call you if you overly love a statue, which is what Photi, denied access to the sanctuary, began to do. Deny a Greek access to a sanctuary, and pump pump go the mighty pistons of destiny and you enter the classic realms of *agonistes*. With the hypothetical head of our Nike installed in his room, the absence of the rest of her — torso, wings, and momentousness — became for Photi a personal infirmity — his malaise.

Photi, we believe, is unique among the thin ranks of glypholepts. Enamored of a statue that is not there, he talks and talks about this statue that is not there. And in his kitchen, above the sink, on a calendar of a year long gone *pfft*, our Nike, outside of human time, stands forever regnant in the Louvre. Forever regnant in the Louvre? asks Photi of himself as he cuts vegetables to boil a soup. Whose is that to decide? Oh, how sweet the French: if ever I visit the Louvre, I might just be allowed a look!

In dreams begins responsibility, we have heard him say, and we think, Yes, Photi our poet would say something admirable like that.

Photi, we know, has seen in the morning haze and evening moonlight the Nike's phantom grandeur rising like the Mary of Jesus above the grave. We know because he has told us so. And we know that at night in bed when a breeze-induced tree branch tap-taps his window, he hears wing-thuds. We know because when a branch tap-taps our windows, we too hear wing-thuds.

Even so, we wield the epithet glypholept on Photi as we would wield a stick on a mule.

What to do about Photi and his glypholepsy?

Take him to a psychiatrist in Athens or Vienna? Hire a sculptor to carve his mother's face on the rock and be done with it? Send him to the Louvre as the hunchbacked and the sick are sent for healing to Lourdes, the shrine of the Virgin Mary?

In the smoky councils of our coffeehouses and tavernas it is decided: the Louvre-as-Lourdes cure. A therapeutic visit by Photi to our fallen angel on the landing. When the wings of his spirit meet the wings of hers, perhaps he will see that to be so enamored of a statue is a sublime misfortune not to be suffered by a grown man, and through some miracle of healing — a walk in the rains of Paris? a laying on of hands by an affronted burly Louvre guard? — our Photi will return to us unburdened.

Photi, we know, has not put by even a little for such a pilgrimage, so from village to village he pedals his bike, a fishbowl tied in a Turk's-head knot to its handlebars. Into the bowl we drop our coin and paper drachmas; when full, a roundtrip Olympic Airways ticket to Paris.

With each donation, Photi rings his bike bell, dring-dring, and advises: Enjoy the day; at night, find love.

His own as the aphorism may be, Photi, alas, is no exemplar. Little is there in each day that he enjoys, and when at night will he find love?

When the drachmas, far off or near, fall into Photi's bowl and we hear his bell register them, we think of Photi as a fare collector and ourselves as passengers on the deck of a cruiser or a clipper called *Anthropos*. Photi does that to us, without even trying.

Of Plato it was said that no matter which direction you were going, Plato was always coming back. Of Photi we say, No matter which way you are going, Photi is pedaling up behind you.

At Easter, when the news arrives that Christ has risen, we respond, Verily, and so when Photi says to us, "The Nike will rise and come back to us," we say, Verily, Photi, verily.

In our tavernas and coffeehouses, where there are not two Samothracians who cannot outpoint him at three-handed pinochle, Photi walks by the tables and gently goads, "Was Samothrace not once a mighty sea power, the site of the famous mysteries, where initiates earned rings, and King Philip met Olympia and sired Alexander?"

Verily, we answer, and notice that Photi's fly lacks a button.

"Does not the *Iliad* say that Poseidon, from the highest peak of Samothrace, beheld the battle of Troy?"

Yes yes, we respond, and demand, Deal the cards.

If Photi were a buffoon, we would laugh. Since he is the son of Sappho and Pindaros Anthropotis, we listen.

Photi calls us *adelphia mou*, my sisters and brothers. *"Adel-phia mou,"* he asks, "is this our Victory's legacy? Souvenir posters and cheap figurines?"

No, say we, no.

"Do we know her legacy?" he asks, and Yes, we answer, Verily.

Photi we know loves the word *verily*, and we know an-other word he loves. It is a sextosyllabic he pumps from us when he exhorts, "And in the noble lexicon of our fore-fathers, what word does this legacy go by?"

"Epanapatrismos," we respond, and he, pleased by our concord, affirms each melodious syllable: *"E-pan-a-pa-tris-mos."* Repatriation.

Under our mustaches, out of Photi's hearing, we men

say: Repatriation? The waters first will close over us. We women say: Too much was Photi with his mother, too much.

Onward bikes Photi, his legs pumping, his lament never lapsing: "We have become an island of microwave ovens and liquid soap. Our victories are Nintendo games and 'Star Trek' reruns. Our spirit drowses; if it heard a reveille, it would blink and go back to sleep."

No, no, we protest, but truth is truth. Once an island fears its soul is expiring, it begins to breathe bubbles and feels submersible. Atlantis-itis sets in, that dread of Greek islands, second only in imagined horror to massacre, Turkish style. Along our coasts and up and down our mountainsides, when fierce winds rage, we say, Better to be blown away than to sink. So we listen to Photi and drop in drachmas. Dring-dring.

Our cheesemaker assays the bowl of drachmas, decides it leaks, but again he feeds the fishbowl, and asks Photi if our Nike could speak for herself, what would she call him, brother, father, husband, or son?

Photi, a feta connoisseur, carves himself a nugget of goat cheese, answers, "My heart's desire," and pedals on.

Our baker tells Photi that he prays that our Nike be not the object of such obsession in Photi's thoughts. Photi, passing up a Francophilic croissant, accepts an indigenous powdered pastry, and responds that the baker and his donkey, which brings mountain thorn for his fires, are, if they will pardon the comparison, brothers in resignation. The baker is penitent, drops a dozen-plus coins into the bowl, and on rolls Photi to reach and beseech each one of us.

Photi is playing a tune on us, and we like it. Though for generations our belief in repatriation has been petering out, now we feel it petering in.

Around and around our habitual shores he pedals, sowing feelings of loss, abandonment, desecration. "Is our Nike a shoe for basketball or our almost sacred heirloom?" Our almost sacred heirloom, we proclaim, and drop more drachmas, dring-dring.

As Photi bikes away, our tongues make a phonetically pure Greek sound established over millennia to urge a horse, a pathetic horse, onward. So as Photi rides and rings his bell, he hears all along our shores and up and down our mountainsides our prodding tcheek-tcheek.

Dring-dring and tcheek-tcheek.

❧ ❧

On the night the leak-prone fishbowl finally proves it has a bottom, we assemble at our countinghouse, a taverna where a bouzouki plays the American tune "Dream." Photi's first and second secret flames commandeer the bowl, spread the drachmas on a table, and with their diamond rings of stentorian carats blaring it to him that matrimony had raised them to a level of life he could never have raised them to, they total. Because these ring-flashing hands are the hands Photi asked for in marriage, it pleases both women, when not busy with their husbands, to do little tasks for him, such as sewing on a button, and though it is shameful of us to say so, we think they wish he would not blame himself for the lasting wounds of his heart, because they fancy for themselves the credit.

When the drachmas overtop the Olympic Airways fare, the house sends wine and ouzo all around and the women kiss Photi's smooth-shaven cheek as they would the cheek of a long-bearded priest.

~ *3* ~

ON A SUNNY MORNING we give Photi a dockside sendoff.
It is the luscious week of summer when the hibiscus and fig
trees flower. From our villages and slopes we come with our
susceptibilities and our worry beads to witness the blessing
of Photi.

A priest, black-robed and long-bearded, blesses Photi
"on this almost religious quest of our hearts" and sprinkles
the prow with holy water.

Photi crosses himself and puts on his bank guard's cap.
He wears his blue pinstriped go-to-weddings suit and tie.
We know the weddings the suit and tie have gone to, and we
know the pain of the also-ran he felt at the church steps,
adding his little handfuls to the geysers of thrown rice and
grain.

He boards the small twice-a-day boat to the mainland,
the first leg of the journey to Paris. The boat is blue and
white, the air-of-heaven colors of its wind-tickled Greek flag.

Photi stands at the bow, his face a coin, a silver tetra-
drachm, of epic determination. His valise is his father's, the
timeless purple-blue one his father, when he eloped to
America, left behind for Photi with just these things in it:
his father's hair dryer, stuck on Cool, and his mother's wedding wreath, every silvery bead of which still gleams, says
Photi, as if a drop of dew is on it.

Photi, we jest, you have underpacked for Paris. No
skyhook, no battering ram? The Louvre, be assured, is no
henhouse.

Insofar as this amusement goes, we enjoy Photi's departure, but in our hearts we feel an ancient dread. It is born of
the works of Aeschylus and Sophocles, at the end of which
audiences dry their tears and adjudge: what had to happen,
happened.

We wave farewell.

He does not wave back. Somewhere he saw it written
that one-sandaled Jason and lyre-playing Orpheus did not
wave back. Nor did the heroes who sailed to Troy to free
Helen from the thieving arms of Paris.

Photi accords us instead an inexperienced V-for-Victory
sign and catches hold of his cap, which the air is about
to take.

Enjoy the day, we are advised; at night, find love.

Because we love Photi, we say that God had a hard time finding the clay and cheese to make him.

Put a sea around the Louvre and it would be an island and then we could vie, toe to toe, with it. No one, of course, is an island, but sent to the Louvre, our Photi comes close.

Our spirit, we feel, has flown Olympic Airways with Photi — resides, wings aflap, inside him. Life on Samothrace now seems unconcentrated. Each day we wonder how is Photi vying? We miss him. The falling silent of his bell has saddened us. No bike, no dring-dring, no exhortations. With Photi in Paris we run onto each other's heels because at work and home our heads turn to watch the glimmers of the sea for sign of him.

Each day the boat with Photi twice not on it. Odysseus

was overdue by twenty years. Overdue by one week, Photi,
we say, must return soon — his bird feeder is on empty, his
nightlight will burn out. Although we do not say it, we feel
it: if Photi were to vanish, our sparkling streams would become a poor trickle.

Today, one of sunshine, we see the boat again with no
Photi on it, but at the bow, in white toreador pants and
mauve blouse, stands an auburn-haired woman in sunglasses; untanned, she is tall and slender, severely beautiful.
She wears a wide beribboned hat.

One glance at her, we know her for a stranger, not a
tourist. One glance at us, she likes how our faces will photograph; we, not she, are guests.

On deck with her is a crew, four tanned young men, her
technicians. They have the look of a musical band much in
thrall to their leader. "Are you Frank Sinatra?" a boy on the
dock calls out to a thin, aristocratic-looking man with the
crew. He wears the nineteenth-century costume of a consul.
"Acteur," the man replies semi-divinely.

She and they disembark. Except for the *acteur*, who
breathes only sparingly, they like our air, our sun, our pro-
pensity for wine, song, and dancing *Opa!* with arms about
each other's shoulders. "Wisconsin, Here I Come," reads
a sticker on her luggage.

She is Susanna Regas, an *Americana* of Greek descent, here to direct the discovery scene for a PBS documentary titled "Silhouette of Victory."

PBS? we ask.

"Public Broadcasting Service," she answers. "No commercials. Limited budget."

Documentary? we ask.

"Real people and events," she responds. "No Mickey Mouse."

Susanna, fit forties, looks to us like a long night of love. Her eyeliner is drawn beyond the lid in the Jocasta manner, and her lips are salmon-hued, come-pay-Mother-a-kiss lips. We believe that wherever this woman goes, she has a hard time reaching home again.

She has won acclaim presenting on television, in twenty-six minutes, the heroic but pathetic stories behind the world's revered artworks. El Greco's *Burial of Count Orgaz* was one, Michelangelo's *David* another. This we hear from her minions, who wear white sneakers and tight khaki short pants and call her Mother. They carry her luggage and her laptop; they stack her cameras. They stay in her view. They have the look of naked runners she has put the stopwatch to. Mother knows what they do. They know what to do for Mother. She pairs with none of them.

When she removes her hat a minion carries it, and her frizzy auburn hairset emerges; a tremor of efficacy, her hair is not even a once-a-day perturbation. Though sunglasses conceal them, her eyes, we believe, are blue-green and beautiful, and though she is of no large account at her blouse, it would please a crowd of men to watch her skip rope. When she walks down our cobblestones to look us over, she is already a camera, and we are her subjects.

Outside the hotel, her minions gather the curious. She announces: she will hire diggers, six of them — Samsons, with chests bared — and she needs seven shovels.

Seven shovels, six Samsons? we ask.

"One is for Monsieur Charles François Champoiseau," she says, and presents for our scrutiny the uppity French *acteur* holding a heroic stance beside her.

Champoiseau, we murmur to each other, slightly snarling.

"Philhellene," assures the *acteur*.

Hide your valuables, whispers one of us to all of us.

Champoiseau dig? we ask Susanna Regas.

"Digs and hollers Eureka!" she answers.

She will audition diggers at the sanctuary.

"Where is the sanctuary?" she asks. "Is it guarded?"

5

O<small>N THE BOAT THE NEXT MORNING</small>, a somber-faced, head-bandaged Photi arrives. No Nike bedecks the prow, his fingers give no Victory sign; his cap is held like a penitent's in his hand. His bandage is Foreign Legionnaire, showier than the one the sanctuary bump begot.

We had hoped for an unbandaged Photi, an exorcised Photi. We cluster at dockside to greet him. The child-daughter of his first secret flame is here to present him a garland of artificial, nonallergenic peonies.

He disembarks, wearing the clothes he left with, but not the savoir-faire.

We smell the marble on him.

The child presents the peonies and earns a downhearted kiss from Photi.

"*Adelphia mou*," he begins sadly, "I pay you the words I owe you."

Dismayed by his tone, we brace for an apologia.

Photi Anthropotis speaks:

I find the Louvre. A fortress. I venture toward it. I enter its glass pyramid. I feel like a tomb explorer. I reach the Hall of Antiquities. Marbles worthy of a look, but I have come on business.

There, atop the wide marble stairs, she stands. In half-light. Our Nike. Supremely alone.

I climb slowly toward her, my senses swimming, my heart a rhythmus of hammer strokes. At eight feet tall, she seems four-thirds the size of life. My eyes carry up along her torso, her thighs strong, her midriff colossal ... carry up across the feathery expanse of her wings ... wings that must, at last, justify themselves.

She is like a poise of the spirit, and yet there — feet at rest on the stone prow of a nonexistent ship — she is captive, a *prisonnier*, and she has a pallor. A pallor, my friends.

I stand on the landing, within hands' reach.

I look high, to the large oval skylight above those wings. Oh, how the sky would own her, give her future! I look back at her and think of us who would own her, give her future. My eyes become moist.

How wind-whipped she is, how brave, standing there with bold heart and steady knees. Through my tears I see a heartbeat. I stand motionless at this moment of miracle. A breast-moving heartbeat! A warrior woman's heartbeat.

She seems to know I have come in the cause of her deliverance. Though she is armless, I feel embraced; though she is headless, I hear her whisper.

We catch our breaths listening to Photi. We chorus: What did she whisper? What did she whisper? We become expansive as the value of our shares shoots up.

Photi whispers to us, "O Island that dreams of me, *ela, ela*." Come, come.

We gasp. Our Photi, hearing things? His glypholepsy worsening, not bettering?

Photi goes on:

I stand on tiptoe. I give her ankle a lingering, chaste feel.

"*Pas permis,*" I hear from behind. A feminine voice, trained to assert.

My hand remains on the marble — *our* marble, which, alas, our frosts never whiten and our summer breezes never cool.

"Not permissible," I hear.

I do not withdraw my fingers.

A clutching hand overtops my hand.

Adelphia mou, can you believe: the ankle of our Nike not permissible to Photi Anthropotis?

The guard has large eyes, sunflowers that glare. She is short, roundish, and wears trousers. Not long ago she was very young. Her glare is a cold caryatid's. The landing is her jurisdiction, and I, in not so shiny shoes, stand in it.

I do not withdraw my hand. Is not the deployment of my hand mine to decide? My tears stop. France, I say to myself, must never see you cry. I glare back at this cold sunflower.

Her hand pulls mine, ejects it from our Nike as if eliminating a contaminant.

I do not accept this kindly. I utter a genetic Greek *Mba!*

"Rules, monsieur," she says.

It is the lot of guards, I respond, and she looks away from me, from my indignation.

Visitors pass by us — pilgrims with cameras and camcorders. Flash click and whir, flash click and whir.

Crowd control hums inside this guard's system.

I carry no camera. I carry an island.

I admire the guard's blue uniform, its buttons, its trouser crease. I like her cap, its no-tilt, no-monkey-business. But her fragrance! It is *parfum du prison!*

I stand between our Nike and the guard, she in her stance, I in mine.

The statue has a pallor, I accuse.

The guard differs: "Her coloring is champagne sorbet."

A pallor, I insist, and she replies, "She has her slant of sunlight. Do you prescribe fresh air and exercise?"

She steps away; she has been too sweet and patient with me.

The statue is in my dreams, I say to her. My picture of Nike is an icon in my kitchen.

"I saw your tears," she answers, and steps back to me. She says, "Some find the statue monotonously triumphant."

How do you find her? I ask.

"Monotonously triumphant," she confesses, and then she looks at me and says, "Baudelaire said that everything that is not perfection should hide its head."

We will take her back then, I offer.

"Are you *Grec?*"

Samothracian.

"Samothrace," she says, as if it belongs on a list of imaginary places.

My sisters and brothers, this annoys me. The island of Saint Helena did not sound so unnecessary to Napoleon as did Samothrace to this woman.

She is ours, I say, not unpleasantly, yet strongly.

"Ours?" she repeats, as if no French equivalent exists.

Oui, I say, not yours, and she smiles at such an amusing assertion.

"Have you come to take her home?"

Oui, I reply, and she asks, "How large is your *cuisine?*"

It annoys me that she sees me as a pathetic person with a kitchen, not as d'Artagnan awaiting his hour to strike.

She tells me, "All Samothrace should know, in the hands of *la France, la Victoire de Samothrace* has been an *objet* of special mercy."

Merci beaucoup, I rebound with due courtesy, and I tell her: Our Nike is as inalienably ours as the Arch de Triumph is inalienably yours.

"L'Arc de Triomphe," she corrects.

Nee-kee of Sam-o-thra-kee, I correct, and then I declare: One Victory is sufficient for Paris.

Up rises her consternation, like a cat's. "Monsieur, here she is the world's. There she'd be . . . but yours."

Her 'but yours' pours salt on our wound.

Robbery, I accuse. *Kidnappeur.*

"Instinctive clutching," she prefers. "Very French."

The pillaging of pirates is instinctive clutching too, I reply with all possible due courtesy.

"And what do you guard?" she retaliates. "A bank?"

A grave, I answer.

"For a man like you to stand guard, it must be a very famous grave."

Adelphia mou, flattery I've suffered before, but not French *flatterie.* I inhaled it. Now to me she looks petite. Now this woman with short brown hair and a gruff grasp seems not at all to have been nursed as a child by a she-bear.

I tell her that archeologists call the grave the findspot.

"Ah," she perceives, "the spot where Her Eminence was disentombed from oblivion."

You have a way of expression, I say.

"We are both," she says, "in the service of *notre* Nee-kee of Sam-o-thra-kee."

By her exhibitionistic Greek pronunciation she seeks to placate me, but *notre,* the Gallic "our," is irksome. Notre Dame, *oui,* I say; Notre Nike, no.

"Yes, yours," she replies. "Yes, ours."

Oh, my companions, is it not ours alone to call our Nike ours? I stare at the guard and think of the useless decades of diplomatic tug of war in the cause of repatriation.

I think of the cold reiterations from Paris to Athens that possession is nine points of the law.

I bristle. I consider the guard. On her uniform, not a button lacking; on her face, years of loneliness. My Thracian chestnut eyes skirmish with her stubborn French hazel ones.

"Think of her *there*," she says, "on your island. What was she but buried broken wings and bones? *Here*, look at her, enjoying complete classic health on her royal perch — Victoire Voluptueuse, seen by millions in her eternal moment of high bliss. The bore."

To myself I say: Photi, here is a woman plagued by heartburn.

I tell her, She is yours like the bones of Napoleon are ours.

Brusquely she says, "Possession, monsieur, is nine points of the law, and the guards of *le Musée du Louvre* are the tenth."

Oh, not again — that obnoxious nine points of the law! Up rises my ire. My mother, you know, did not permit me low colloquialisms. So I let out with some resonance an ingrained response — not our handed-down ancient one: Barbarians! Barbarians! I let out a *Kyrie eleison*.

Visitors at *le Musée du Louvre* are tolerated only to make

a fine front for the artworks, and a resonant "Lord have mercy" is not *le Musée du Louvre's* idea of a fine front.

"Silence, please, monsieur," she demands. "This is not a church."

A prison, I respond unsoftly, and I say it in French too, giving *prison* an almost surly sizzle.

Although in the male phalanx of guards that appears two of them have a ballerina's definition to their shoulders, they are all quashers and make a large landing look half its size.

Another doubly fervent *Kyrie eleison* escapes from me.

"Samothracian," she explains to the guards, as if we are a harmless, little-known subspecies.

I receive no respectful greeting. They scrutinize me, await further insolence.

She says to the guards, "Monsieur shouts 'Lord have mercy.' Perhaps he believes God to be deaf."

I forget my upbringing. I forget I am Photi Anthropotis, for whom dignity and more dignity are the twin blessings each night I pray for. I raise my voice and hurl at them: Grave robbers! *Scandale! Scandale!*

Advised to move on, I consider the advice. With all possible courtesy I inform the guard: Madame, I believe God not to be deaf.

"Mademoiselle," she corrects, and the guards laugh their uncongenial French laugh.

I walk away.

She calls out to me, "Monsieur, *pardon*. My job is not to make a *touriste* feel a trespasser."

I reply, Mademoiselle, without a grave, there can be no resurrection.

୬ ୬

The next day, a cloudy one, I visit *la tombe de Napoléon*, under the gold dome of the Invalides. The crypt is an indestructible edifice, tons of red porphyry, under which Napoleon's bones lie sealed forever. I file past. What could you do with the bones anyhow? Hold them hostage? Return our Nike — or we grind the bones?

Photi, I ask myself, do two thefts make a right? How far you have drifted from the probity taught you by your mother. How would she, in her grave, countenance such an act? Would not her own bones feel your transgression and wish to put the birch once more to your posterior?

I walk down the Champs-Élysées. Even our Elysium and

its fields, they want! I stand at *l'Arc de Triomphe*. It, at least, is penetrable. The *matri*-arch of Paris. Napoleon's idea of triumph — a womb, with *haut*-reliefs. But what can you do with *l'Arc de Triomphe?* Climb it and shout to Paris at peak hour, shout *Voilà*, I jump? They would only photograph you and put you on their postcards.

I feel dejected. I walk back to *le Musée du Louvre*. No, a henhouse it is not; it is a Bastille, a walled Troy. Once a fortress and then a palace, the palace became a fortress again, a vault. I dislike the air of suzerainty, the smell of loot and colonial clout. I stroll the halls, the *salons* and *salles*. I inspect the paintings, the *objets d'art*, the stone phantoms, all seemingly produced with a finger snap out of a *chapeau*.

At marbles belonging to the noblest realms of sculpture, I pause.

The Cariatides.

Metopes of the temple of Zeus.

Friezes of the Parthenon.

The Aphrodite de Milo. The Miloans say she is a creation more beautiful than our Nike. Miloans! Islanders, what do you expect!

Salle de Phidias.

Salle de Praxitèle.

Salle de Corinthe.

I sigh: the glories of Greece of Paris.

I approach our Nike, serene in her small space of light, aloof though alluring, ageless though two thousand years old. Had she a cheek, I would put health in it.

The guard is there. She watches me. She has graver doubts about me now.

I have graver doubts about myself. I feel like a low sham. Repatriator? Or just a bothersome visitor, a dreamer? No plan, no tactics. Defeat again. *Cocorico!* If my defeats were roosters, oh the cacophony!

I touch the ankle of our Nike. I want the guard to know I relinquish not a toe, not the least inch.

"Pas permis," I hear again, and again I refuse to withdraw my hand. Again her hand grasps mine.

Though I am a second-time offender, her grasp is less gruff, less a grasp than a clasp. I perceive something surprising in it. It has a dance-with-me readiness. Photi, I say to myself, I cannot but suspect that this woman has peculiar private rules of her own.

She releases my hand and looks away, steps away.

My touch of the Nike ankle may linger for as long as I wish.

I confess to you, *adelphia mou,* that the touch of her hand on my hand was not unpleasant. But think not otherwise: it is our Nike who enchants me, our Nike whose spirit has enheartened me in my darkest months and, in my brightest moments, inspired my soul and thoughts.

I remove my hand. I kneel, face upward to our Nike. I gaze out beyond her wings into the darkening sky. O God, I implore, if it has befallen me to repatriate our Nike, allow some sign to reach me.

Directly from my lips to the ears of God to my upturned nose — a raindrop! Through the skylight. A second drop drips. This too on my nose, lest doubt exists that God has perfect hearing, perfect aim. When a third raindrop anoints me, I rise and shout, Rain! A deluge!

We feel a thrill. God has visited rain on Photi. Rain augurs well, does it not? Are not the great catches of our trawlers preceded by rain? Did it not rain pitchforks when a bullet blew the brains of Mussolini and Hitler sucked poison from his ring?

Go on, Photi, we urge, go on.

Photi goes on:

The guard quickly approaches, with the phalanx behind her.

"A thin drizzle," she apologizes to calm me. "A glazier will come tomorrow and repair it."

Ah, we exclaim, *deus ex machina!* The Fates provide! A hole in the skylight. Photi up a ladder to the roof. Reconnaissance. Undermining the Louvre from the top. Photi peering down the skylight like a beardless Pantocrator, or a cat burglar, devising tactics. Pluck her out by helicopter? Oh, what a dream catch that would be! Our Nike in a fishnet! Photi piloting a whirlybird, our Nike dangling from it! Transported in a stout Samothracian net, winging and swinging in scherzo over France and Italy, across Greece — cheered on from the mountains and valleys, from the ships at sea, hailed wildly, ecstatically, all the airborne way to Samothrace.

All wonderful, we remind each other, except that Photi does not fly, does not drive even.

But oh how we love an epic sung to us! Go on, Photi, we urge, go on. Just don't marry our daughters.

On he goes:

Mademoiselle, I tell the guard, our Nike, as you see her, descends from the summit of heaven to celebrate a victory at sea, not to suffer the rains of Paris. I protest this unkind treatment, and I object to your glaring henchmen, whose eyes give me the Victory sign with one finger.

"Move on, monsieur," the guard orders. "Move on."

Though never have I bellowed, I come shamefully close:
Move on? Photi Anthropotis does not move on!

The phalanx encloses me.

Seized by my shoulders, I am escorted down the majestic stairway, through the Hall of Antiquities, and out into the night and its downpour.

❧ ❧

The next morning, I am outside *le musée* when the glazier arrives. He sees my cap and takes me to be an inspector. He sets up his ladder. I look at those rungs, row upon row of them — up, up the mast to the great light of day.

The glazier climbs. I follow slowly, lead-footed; I have heart-jumping jitters. Oh, what a long way I have come to this ladder, to this pane of glass — come from trailing mullet, come from the little jounces of our Aegean. Why do I climb? I ask myself. Have I a plan? Even the pigeons have a plan: occupy every rooftop and drop on it and from it. Nothing have I, nothing but a wildly throbbing heart and a loosened sphincter. And — oh, no! — it is Thursday. No days call down curses on my head like Thursdays. Yet I climb, my knees yogurt, my brain asking why, why, and my heart answering: I climb not because our Nike is here, I climb because I am here, Photi Anthropotis, light and humanity.

I must confess to you, my sisters and brothers, that I sometimes fancy that the Fates bestowed on me the name Photi, and by so doing, placed within me an inner luminescent something, to be, well, at least a glint in His almighty glory. But the truth is — I know it and you know it — I was saddled with the name by my mother, who saw an insufficiency of love and light in her life until I, like a bulb, popped up.

The glazier attains the top. Breathing in gulps, I attain the top. The same sky over me, over our Nike. I have entered her firmament. I face all that sky. So much there to be loose in — to arise to and be free, free from heartache and catastrophe. I remain on the ladder. I peer down through the skylight. I see our goddess, entombed. I see her seldom seen upper plumage of wings. Oh, if only they were wings I could ride, ride! I see her neck, her headlessness. Who needs a head when she has more than human consciousness?

The glazier examines the caulking, finds the leak, and

of course, being French, he proclaims, Eureka! My ears hear him only distantly, because my stomach has renounced me, and my legs on the ladder won't stay put. I am s-w-a-y-ing and s-w-o-o-n-ing. I fall. I hit the glass and my own self-disgusted reflection in it. I wake up on the level white space of a hospital bed.

We gasp. Oh, God! Our Photi rushed in a siren-wailing ambulance to a hospital. Go on, Photi, we urge, go on. Just don't marry our daughters.

On goes Photi:

I hear remote fog signals. Inside the bandage my brain is a warbling universe. I perceive a blue blur, like a water lily beside my bed. I smell a fragrance. *Parfum du prison.*

The guard. In her cap. Why is she here? I ask myself. *Rapprochement?*

She says to me, "Hubristic heroes falling from heights, it is very Greek."

I am silent.

"Pride goeth before a fall," she says.

I ask myself: Has this woman come to recite a list of archaic exhortations?

My vision clears. The blue — it is her uniform, not a button lacking.

"Monsieur, are you on a mission to liberate the Nike?"

I do not answer.

"It would be *excentrique*," she says. "*Le Musée du Louvre* is a fortress. Troy would be easier. The bones of Napoleon would be easier."

The bones of Napoleon? I ask.

"Buried under tons of red porphyry," she says, "and yet on Wednesday the doors opened for visitors and there, head against the crypt, a man was sleeping."

I ask, By sleeping there, he warmed the bones?

"He sought inspiration," she tells me. "Robbers of cemeteries doze among the graves to find inspiration. Champoiseau, it is said, slept at the Sanctuary of the Great Gods and thereby was inspired to dig. The sleep of the sanctuary is a kind of divination, believed in by people with large dreams and small sense."

Who, I ask, would steal the bones of Napoleon? And she answers, "A provocateur, monsieur. To extract some treasure from France."

A provocateur, our Photi? We laugh at what this woman has said to him. Our Photi, a poet maybe, but a provocateur!

Was this person apprehended? I inquire, and she tells

me, "The guard roused the man and he apologized, took foot, and fled. He was a sad man, wore a blue suit and cap, like the one left behind on the roof of *le musée*."

Has *le musée* sent you to question me?

"I have come to return it," she says, and upends my cap on the bed. She asks, "Inside the lining, why a floor plan of *les Invalides?* With the vault of Bonaparte marked by skull and crossbones?"

I do not answer.

"The man," she says, "is believed to be the same lost soul who later that day wormed his way into *l'Arc de Triomphe* and scaled the top."

We are aghast. Photi to the top!

On goes Photi: I ask the guard, Why would this man scale *l'Arc?*

"To elicit sympathy."

Sympathy? I ask.

"For a cause," she says. "This *excentrique* stood there, a small de Gaulle, as if wanting to shout something to all of Paris. But he was silent — he just remained there, ashamed of himself. He was carried out feet and shoulders, like an Easter lamb, and warned never to return."

We are distressed. Our Photi ejected, shown no courtesies. Did they think he would pee on their arch? Photi, go on, go on.

Photi goes on:

The guard asks, "Monsieur, have you come to descend on Paris like a plague?"

You ask many questions, I say to her.

"Little pilgrim," she says to me, "I ask one question: Do I drive you home with me, or do I call the police?"

꒰ ꒱

Photi's narrative stops. He has seen an unknown woman in the crowd, sitting at a table under an acacia tree. A woman in a wide beribboned hat, a laptop in her lap. She has been sipping an ouzo and listening.

He no longer wants to talk to us. He tells us we will hear the rest of the story in the tavernas and coffeehouses.

Yes, we say, later we will raise high our cups and glasses and hear the rest of the story.

Photi leaves behind his purple-blue suitcase. He walks toward the woman and asks, Who are you?

She looks up from her laptop and answers, "I am your Trojan horse."

PART TWO

❧ 1 ❧

IN OUR TAVERNAS AND COFFEEHOUSES, Photi does not really tell us the rest of the story. He is embarrassed, of course, but treated to ouzos and demitasses, he intimates, he implies, he lets slip.

So we treat ourselves to the rest of the story, cup to cup, glass to glass. The tale becomes breeze-perpetuated, like a sail, a mighty galleon, gaining detail and currency as it puts in at every taverna, every coffeehouse.

The guard's name is Gabrielle, and yes, he went home with her. Why?

Aah, *romanzo!* What else? Down goes Photi once more, we fear. Another rebuff, another scar? Can Photi, in Paris, where four-fifths of the inhabitants die of grief, find at last the bride we all wish for him?

In her apartment, Gabrielle pours wine. She lives alone with a snow-white cat, which maintains an existential attitude toward Photi's thin-socked feet.

Out of the world's eye now, out of their caps, Gabrielle and Photi sit close to each other on her divan. He admires the stylish cut of her hair, the comeliness of her nape. She admires his nobly shaped nose, his compassionate chestnut eyes. They listen to the night sounds of Paris and the sad ballads of Charles Aznavour. The elegiac grandeur of his songs draws them closer; they hold hands, intertwine fingers; they dare to press cheeks.

She ejects the tape. It is time for Gabrielle's own sad story.

Photi befriends the cat, fondles its ear, and listens.

Gabrielle is the lone daughter of a nonsurviving wine merchant and a nonsurviving airline stewardess. She had a suitor or two long ago, but neither one proposed marriage, nor even romance. Life? She longed to be like her mother, a stewardess, tall and thin, adept at giving men puncturing looks of superiority. Sooner than a stewardess, Gabrielle could become a clown in a *cirque*. Or become a guard. Nine years a guard, nine years in ministry to a monument. Doldrums, day after day. More organized tours, more droves of tourists mounting the Daru stairs, more cameras clicking, more couples in love for her to envy. Men pass by and do not see her, handsome men with perfect vision. Is this to be her fate, decade after decade, invisibility in a fishbowl? Does not life promise some fulfillment? Does not *la Victoire* herald some bright tomorrow?

Photi listens sadly. He knows little about bright tomorrows.

Where, she asks him, is her cavalier, her d'Artagnan? If not some gallant prince like the one who comes upon Cinderella's slipper on a stairway, if not the dashing one who sits atop that immemorial white horse, at least a baker, a butcher, a wine-barrel maker.

"Ah, Gabrielle," sighs Photi, "you are lonely and *mélancolique*."

She sighs profoundly at the truth of this and says, "Your marble madonna, too, is lonely and *mélancolique*. We are sisters. One spirit. I have the head, she the heart. Each day I say to myself, Gabrielle, you are fodder for a convent."

Photi laughs. "You, in a wimple?"

"The statue and I share a wish," she says.

"A wish for what?" he asks.

"A quiet departure by coach," she answers. "The triumph of Cinderella."

The thought of triumph, even Cinderella's, excites Photi.

"She was beautiful," reminds Gabrielle. "A coach for the beautiful always comes." Somberly she asks, "What's to admire about a short, round woman in trousers? What's to admire . . . ?"

"Gabrielle," says Photi, "you are petite and pretty and have the grip of a thin woman. And your uniform — pressed so neatly and not a button lacking."

She pours him more of her father's wine.

Passion colors his cheeks. He leans toward her, he kisses her — a Louvre guard!

She kisses him. It is a kiss she would give d'Artagnan.

"Ah, Gabrielle, you are an angel without wings, and if I had your picture in my kitchen, there would be two women of monumental beauty there."

Flattered, she loosens his necktie and asks, "Monsieur Photi, the icon of *la Victoire*, is it above your sink?"

He nods.

"Among the secrets of your heart, is this sink the lost fountain of the sanctuary?"

Photi feels found out.

"And do you at times *feel* the Nike, feel her in flight, and that she and you are apparitions, mythic figures with wings?"

He confesses with a nod.

"And do you live the rhythms in your body?"

"Yes, yes," he admits, and asks himself: Am I the glypholept or is she?

He rises. To pee. That, too, she perceives, and she indicates the direction of the *cabinet*.

The cat follows him.

Gabrielle shoos the cat.

When he returns, Gabrielle is in her narrow little bedroom and has pulled down the coverlet. On her bed, the cat has occupied a secondary place.

Yes, we excitedly say to each other, Photi was right: the woman has peculiar private rules of her own.

Standing in uniform by her pillows, she awaits him. She, Mademoiselle Sunflower; he, inveigled invader. He comes forward. They embrace. He kisses her neck, her lips. They feel each other's arms, thighs. To facilitate Mister Findspot, she unbuttons her trousers, one two three four. "Not a button missing," she boasts. Then, one two four, she unbuttons him.

Ah, *rapprochement*. Ah, *erotas! Amour!* But is it?

In the tavernas and coffeehouses we embrace that question in all its wholeness.

Oui, some of us answer. For this reason she retrieved his cap from *le* roof and sat with him through the night in *le* hospital. For this reason she allowed him *carte blanche* of our Nike's ankle.

No, some of us answer. True love? Impossible! They are adversaries, obverse sides of a coin, and though Love Conquers All may be writ on some coins, on this, in French and Greek, we see: Up yours, Victory Is Ours.

Telling and retelling the story, we this alone agree on: In a Paris apartment, Photi puts aside his repatriatorship and becomes a dashing d'Artagnan, and Gabrielle puts aside her uniform and becomes *le* dish. She and he are, for one night, maybe two, "together." Odysseus and Calypso. And then, we decide, Photi remembers with a shiver the insatiable sirens of Homer, and he sighs *"Adieu,* my angel" and escapes Paris, and poor, heart-heavy Gabrielle, her cap so set on Photi, returns to the mausoleum on the Seine and stands watch over the Nike as the daily droves of camera clickers mount the Daru stairs.

❧ 2 ❧

CHAMPOISEAU, THE *ACTEUR*, walks about our island as if snakes lurk at his ankles. If this is the man who will discover our Nike, we prefer that she remain undiscovered.

Living the heroic role, Champoiseau is dressed in nineteenth-century consul's garb, pantaloons, vest, and fancy shoes. Amateur antiquarian! He seems to us like a goose and we the golden egg over which he clucks.

Biting a croissant, he carries Susanna's script, "Silhouette of Victory." "It has *splendeur*," he says to our baker, whose donkey is delivering mountain thorn for his fires.

"The croissant?" asks the baker.

"The script," says Champoiseau, and he deplores the croissant: *"Pas authentique."*

"Mba!" exclaims our baker, and pats the donkey's round end. "Here is *splendeur*, here is *authentique*."

In the evening, in the taverna, Susanna works on her

script. Sunglasses off, her eyes *are* blue-green beautiful; leotards off, her legs in a mauve-trimmed sheath dress are more
perfectly calved than the men among us imagined. Her hat
and laptop are on the table.

She has heard the Gabrielle story evolve. She has watched
Photi, drinks placed at his elbow, nod his bandaged head,
bestowing veracity on the details as we worked them out of
him, to titillate our imagination.

Susanna is deep in thought.

As a distinguished PBS writer/director from America,
and with the name of Regas, she is as close as we come
these days to visits by notables.

Our men send flowers to her hotel room and drinks to
her table, though they believe her not to sunbathe nude. A
bouzouki player plucks out a recognizable "Oh! Susanna."

The words are not known to us, so no one sings. So
Susanna sings:

> *Oh! Susanna, don't you cry for me;*
> *I come from Alabama with a banjo on my knee.*

We applaud, we toss kisses.
Photi is drawn to her. He drifts to her table and sits. All

the blows he has been dealt come with him. She continues
to work on her script, which seems like a cake not yet of the
right leaven. He watches her silently. When she looks up at
him, she is pensive.

She says nothing to him that we can overhear.

Photi, we believe, is smitten again, perhaps infatuated.
We know the hoops Photi has jumped through for one vil-
lage princess and another, but we believe for this *Americana*
he will jump even higher. She will eat him. Trojan horse?
Ha! Empty horse, empty talk. She is playing a tune on
Photi.

We watch her put aside her script and place her hands
on Photi's head. She removes his bandage.

His wound is not hideous, merely superficial.

She rises and, disposing of the bandage, announces to
the taverna, "It was a French idea of how a Greek sees his
injuries."

She walks outside and finds a sky of stars. Photi picks
up her hat and her laptop, leaves his bike behind, and walks
with her.

Though Susanna is a foot taller than Photi, in the light
of a circular moon he appears to be a foot taller than
himself.

He seems not so afflicted anymore by the defeats that scar his heart, and not so spooked by poems unwritten, which adhere in a slumped state inside him.

Outside the hotel, she smells the air for atmospheric change. Photi returns her hat and her laptop and bids her goodnight with a kiss of her hand. We have seen Photi kiss the hands of priests and the hands of women, kisses rich in reserve and sentiment, but this one is the kiss of a vassal or a votary.

Just at the moment she turns to depart from him, Photi sighs exuberantly, "Oh, Susanna!"

She steps back to him. For Photi, it is an intimacy and an honor for a woman to step back to him. "Kyrie Photi," she advises, "men with hard-ons call me Mother."

Photi ponders this as he might the iambics of a startling poem. He watches her enter the hotel, then he walks back for his bike and rides the lonely upward path to his house, past the fully supplied wooden bird feeder at his window, which is a window not visible from the road until he goes in and snaps on the light.

❧ 3 ❧

AT THE SANCTUARY, Susanna's minions assemble our
Samsons for Mother's selection.

Photi stands guard near the findspot, his cap set just so,
to eye Susanna when she arrives.

Champoiseau, in consul garb, walks about in the sanctuary as if he has bought it. "Six cocks for Delilah," he implores impatiently, "and we shoot this marvelous scene and
off we go to Pa-ree!"

Our men ignore this Frenchman, but for Susanna they
line up in the sun. They remove their shirts.

She arrives in a mauve-pocketed body suit, chic and
autocratic.

A minion offers her a pencil. Pointed at, each man
turns for her. Not pointed at, the man goes home. She in-
spects their biceps, their chests, how they carry at the fly.
She selects one reluctantly, rejects another unreluctantly.

Those she selects she taps with the pencil, and a minion presents each one a shovel at port arms.

We ask ourselves: Is Susanna a leader of men or a leader-on of men?

When Susanna has one shovel left, she marches to Photi at the findspot. She looks him up and down. He has a button missing, and she knows it. Take his shirt off? Never! "Sooner I would dig my grave than dig for Champoiseau."

"Kyrie Photi," she says, the pencil tapping with nuance on his nose, "I will find a larger role for you."

A tremor runs through Photi. Out in public! This said to him out in public!

Our men exchange glances. Our women feel uncomfortable.

Susanna hires another digger, dismisses the six men, and a minion relieves her of the pencil. She comes back to Photi. Never has a woman dismissed six stalwarts and come to him. She needs a marble fragment, she tells him; the one Champoiseau will turn up with his shovel.

"Champoiseau!" protests Photi. "A Greek turned up the first fragment."

"In Champoiseau's report," says Susanna, "he wrote

that he found it to be the most beautifully shaped woman's breast."

"Braggadocio," denounces Photi.

"Can you help me locate one?" asks Susanna. "A stone that looks like it might be her breast."

Photi's chin goes up and his tongue snicks on his teeth — the ingrained Greek *no.*

"I have heard," she says, "that you have such a fragment. Is this so, Kyrie Photi?"

"A breast?" asks Photi incredulously, as if it would be the last word in the lexicon to describe his marble. "My brothers and sisters told you that the marble which has smiled at me for thirty years at my bedside is a breast?"

"It was, yes, described to me in that fashion."

"How was it described to you?" Photi demands.

"The *parapanisto,*" she replies. "The extra one."

"Never," snaps Photi, as close to a snarl as any of us have seen him. "On saints' days it wears my mother's wreath."

"I'm sure," she says. "And you put on a corsage."

Susanna has learned what we long have known about Photi.

"Too much would be rubbed away," he says. "Find another fragment."

"Greeks!" she scolds. "Chthonian mother cults and siren songs, that's Greeks."

Reprimanded, he is like a boy knowing worse is to come. Coldly, she delivers it: "Kyrie Photi, tonight you will not carry Mother's hat."

~ 4 ~

NIGHT. At the taverna, the ersatz Champoiseau enters, still in consul garb. No one buys him a drink, so he pays for a Metaxa with francs. He sits with Photi, who squirms. Only we know when Photi squirms, for nothing of him moves.

"Let us drink to *la Victoire de Samothrace*," he says, and clinks Photi's glass. The actor drinks, Photi does not.

"The Victory is not exactly the greatest discovery since the Indies," says the Frenchman. "She is *la Victoire populaire*, for the everyday imagination. Marketable, like Monet's lily-pad ashtrays. Oh, ride me, ride me, taunts the queen from her ledge in the Louvre, ride me to the heights, to the final ecstasy, to the presence of God. Ha."

Photi's squirm becomes even more motionless.

The *acteur* is in performance. Melodramatically, he confides, "I fear the statue. How mysterious her connection with human fortunes! So faceless she is, so sly."

Photi would not admit to any feeling he might share with Champoiseau.

"You did not rejoice in Paris," chides Champoiseau.

"Rejoice?" asks Photi. "Why?"

"The grand hussy on the landing."

Photi will not respond to such a provocation.

"Think of it," says Champoiseau. "A hundred shoveled-up fragments, mud-caked and damaged, shipped to France, puzzled out and glued in the workshop of the Louvre to produce — *voilà!* — a monolithic *Victoire*. Thanks to me, Charles François Champoiseau, *découvreur suprême*."

To this Photi will respond. "Discoverer?" he scoffs. "Plunderer."

"In my mind I play and replay the celebrated scene," the *acteur* taunts. "I feel it, breathe it, the thrill *extraordinaire* of finding the first buried fragment. Her breast."

"Breast?" protests Photi. "Donkey shit."

Champoiseau is unfazed. "Like Archimedes, I announce Eureka! For the glory of France! What a *triomphe magnifique!* A shovel, a fragment, a living masterpiece, rising from the grave for all the world to see."

Photi downs his ouzo.

Champoiseau excitedly goes on: "Ah, hear this wonderful line when I, with a shovel's turn, uncover the breast — the world-admired nipple-missing breast: 'Brought up from the dead — dead but still breathing.' That line will rival 'Alas, poor Yorick.'"

Photi finds this man very unpleasant. "Alas," he mocks, "poor Champoiseau did not uncover the first fragment. And it was *not* her breast."

"It is in Champoiseau's report," insists the *acteur*.

"Not her breast! Not her breast! Not her breast!" Photi pounds on the table. "Fantasy," he declares. "Fantasy. Greek diggers dug up the statue. Our grandfathers witnessed it. We heard them proudly tell about it."

The *acteur* ignores this contention and emits an uningratiating titter. "Tomorrow she will be mine," he taunts. "Tomorrow and tomorrow."

With a motion, Photi orders another ouzo. He is annoyed in the extreme. Only we know when Photi is annoyed in the extreme, for he orders ouzo with an imperceptible motion, says nothing, and ceases to breathe.

His silence and immobility annoy Champoiseau. "Greeks!" he grunts. "Always brooding, always a flaw in their craw that kills them." His fist softly touches Photi's chin, a convivial gesture meant to cheer him. "You have given us language, philosophy, poetry, architecture," he says. "One statue more, one less, what matter?"

Photi is silent, unmoving.

Champoiseau opens the script. "Ah, poetry. Ah, grand finale. Listen." He reads:

Champoiseau, 79, in a wheelchair, arrives in the Louvre for his last farewell. He is pushed up the Daru stairs on a plank. The mayor and other dignitaries are gathered on the landing to commemorate, for the last time, his discovery.

CHAMPOISEAU: *Ah, ma Victoire,* I am dying. I brought you up from the dead — dead but still breathing. Now up from the dead you will bring me — still breathing but dead.

Champoiseau rises and climbs atop the prow. He holds his arms up, outstretched like the wings of the Nike. He feels heaven-borne.

CHAMPOISEAU: I rise! I rise!

"Can't you see how wonderful this scene will be?" exclaims the *acteur*. "Champoiseau rising to heaven on the wings of his Victory. Poetry. *Magnifique*. And yet Mother is not happy with the ending."

Photi finally speaks. "Life never ends the way we want it."

"Films do," says Susanna, who has entered. She removes her hat and sits with Photi and Champoiseau. She wears mauve, a safari-cut suit so meant for her that the taverna hushes.

Ouzos are sent to her.

"Mother, cheer him up," Champoiseau pleads. "Monsieur Photi has come back from Paris suffering the twin plagues of France: self-pity and *amour*."

Susanna covers Photi's hand to console him. Her hand comes to Photi with the surprise of a gift. He is pleased. Two hands together can come to be love, can be the beginning of a story, a poem.

"Susanna," he asks, "what is the ending you want?"

"Ascension, Kyrie Photi," she answers. "The grandest theme of humankind."

"*Anabasis*," affirms Photi. "Up."

Although ladders make him woozy, Photi, we know,

loves Up. For him, Up is the place to be, to get to, aspire to. He loves things with wings, butterflies and birds, rooftop poetry. We have seen him walk in his boots to the summit of Fengari, just to stand at the snowy ledge and say hello to himself: Hello, I am here, Photi Anthropotis, here to feed the goats and say to myself yes, today I am out of favor with fortune, but tomorrow! Ah, tomorrow it will be better, it may even be glorious, it will be at least a day without defeat.

"Oh, Susanna," he pleads, "go on. Please, go on."

On she goes: "I did *Burial of Count Orgaz*, a magnificent El Greco. In an open heaven above the earth, we see a crowd of silent faces witnessing the ascension of the dead grandee's soul. The body is merely a surviving vanity these faces do not look at. The ascent to the sublime, life's final exaltation — *that* they witness, *that* they share, and that is the ending I want."

Champoiseau listens, scowling.

She chides the *acteur:* "Champoiseau is but a shovel, an amateur antiquarian, no more worthy of being borne heroically to heaven than the rest of us."

The *acteur* sulks.

"I want soul-stirring, Kyrie Photi," she says. "Joy. Tears.

Anabasis. Mount. Up, up, and away. I want the awe of the sky void of earth."

"The moth crushed is what she wants," says Champoiseau, but Susanna and Photi are not listening. They are "with" each other. Susanna's hand on Photi's is finding something solid in it, something she can use.

"My ascension scene *is* soul-stirring," Champoiseau protests. "It *will* produce tears."

"Actors," says Susanna with exasperation. "A statue upstages them, can they ever live it down?"

Champoiseau rises. Miffed to his gold cufflinks, he exits.

Photi enjoys his exit, even more his absence.

Susanna and Photi. They sit alone now with her hat. Eyes on Photi, hands on Photi, Mother will talk, he will listen. "In every life, a theme. In every great artwork, a theme. I did Michelangelo's *David.* The male as Apollonian perfection. A wonderful story. Michelangelo giving the marble erotic little love pats as he sculpts. He is obsessed by a vision of maleness so sensuous it can best be imagined, not sculpted. Until he does it! Completes the nude and can't let go, can't relinquish his marble god. The inmost wells of Michelangelo's masculinity are sucked so dry by the statue he cannot nourish a pure attachment to any woman. When his *David* is taken from him, installed in the piazza like livestock, the loss kills him. Though he rises high on the scaffold to do the ceiling of the Sistine Chapel, Michelangelo, as a man, has nowhere to go but down."

Photi ponders this. The wells of masculinity? Sucked dry? Installed in the piazza? Many are the times he himself feels sucked dry and installed in our village square.

"Ascension," Photi affirms sadly. "Yes, ascension, Susanna." Then he provides a folk wisdom: "We ride for the fall we take."

Susanna responds, "Back home we say, Aim low, fall low; aim high, fall high; but either way, the north wind blows you down."

Photi knows the blows of fate that can double a man over, and he knows that God, when asked, can give one strength to bear up under those blows. But God cannot intervene every two minutes.

He reveres Susanna, a woman of learning, of PBS, a woman for whom the pain and attainments of others are real.

Photi, we fear, is cucumber in her sandwich.

His face, baking with affection, touches her cheek.

In another moment, she will kiss him, on the lips. The kiss, to us who see it, is something to wonder about. Not a mother's kiss, not a harlot's. What does she seek? we ask each other. His marble? His secret of durable hexameter?

She rises and stands over him. Photi, we believe, would write a poem for Susanna. Oh, had he a lute of fire to sing her beauty and her merits! A romantic to the tip of his penis, he looks into her eyes and quietly sings the two lines of "Oh! Susanna."

We applaud.

Susanna is pleased. She likes this outpouring of local life, likes it that Kyrie Photi is smitten. We know she will once again leave her hat behind. Soon she will have him in short pants, every button buttoned.

She walks out of the taverna.

Photi follows, her wide beribboned hat in his hand.

At the hotel entrance she stops. We watch.

He stands with her, enamored clear to his fingertips. He does not offer the hat. She reaches for it. He will not surrender the hat. "You are an orchid," he says with solemn tenderness. Though pleased, she is stony. She looks away. Her love he wants. To bring her hat to her room he wants.

He stands there waiting, hoping. His fingers winding
the ribbon of the hat are buying time.

"Come, Kyrie Photi, my hat. You will not bring it up
for Mother tonight."

He stands there in blissy defeat.

She waits. We wait. We wonder, will he stand there all
night?

"Susanna ... I love you," he says with emotion. Then
he offers her hat and softly pleads, "Mother ... some
night?"

"On a saint's day," she answers.

This is cruel, but not to Photi. It is a promise.

We ask each other: On that saint's day, will Photi put
on a corsage? But we do not laugh.

Uneasily, into the night sky, we sing the rhyming lines
of "Oh! Susanna" as Photi relinquishes the hat, retrieves his
bike, and pedals home.

❧ 5 ❧

*T*HE DISCOVERY SCENE rehearsal commences. It is 1863.
The cast and director are at the seaside Sanctuary of the
Great Gods. For the camera, brush and weeds are carted
in by the film crew to authenticate the scene, give it an abandoned, unexcavated forlornness. Only traces must exist now
of the elaborate sanctuary, buried by an earthquake fifteen
hundred years before Champoiseau arrives.

The propman carries a stone — the substitute one that
is to be unburied by a shovel. We know the stone. A recent
one, it was uncovered in our cemetery by a gravedigger, who
gave it to a loose widow for a doorstop.

As plump as it is, the stone looks less like a breast than
Photi's bedside marble.

Our young and old find shade to watch. Oh, the years,
the generations we have imagined this scene! Now we will

see it. Our priests, too, have left their fishing poles untended to witness this version of the dead shall rise.

Photi, on guard, sits on a rock above the site. He watches Susanna, in white leotards, mauve tank top, and hat.

She positions her chest-bared Samsons, each with the shovel she has conferred on them.

Champoiseau, bedecked in consul costume, stands on a rise, looking down on the shovels. With a condescending swagger he descends to the level area where the diggers are. With the toe of his shoe he stakes out, in the dust, the area to be excavated.

CHAMPOISEAU: There the Austrians failed. Here the French, time-honored friends of Greece, will succeed. (*He turns to the diggers.*) Homeric men of Samothrace, let the gods hear your shovels, for the glory of Greece.

The digging starts.

FIRST DIGGER: What lip we endure in the name of the glory of Greece.

SECOND DIGGER: Amateur antiquarians wear fancy shoes.

THIRD DIGGER: The Frenchman pays in francs.

FOURTH DIGGER: *Doxa patris.* Glory to our country.

ALL DIGGERS (*resignedly*): *Doxa patris.*

CHAMPOISEAU (*slyly*): *Doxa patris.*

The digging continues.

Champoiseau, leaning on his shovel, watches.

Digging sounds continue as the narrator (Susanna) reads:

Our grandfathers saw the Frenchman with the fancy shoes. They were paid by him to dig. They felt the excitement of discovery. They heard the cries of exultation.

Champoiseau, wielding his shovel, strikes a buried object. He digs. He wrests from the ground a round marble fragment. He clutches it.

CHAMPOISEAU (*shouting excitedly*): Eureka! Eureka!

The diggers run to crowd around Champoiseau. He clutches the marble passionately to his chest.

CHAMPOISEAU (*shouting*): A breast! A breast!

ALL DIGGERS: Our Nike! Our Nike!

CHAMPOISEAU (*possessively*): My Nike! My Nike! Brought up from the dead — dead but still breathing.

The diggers look at each other, perplexed.

Photi angrily shouts, "Stop!"

Susanna raises her hand and listens to him protest: "Champoiseau did not find the fragment. It was not a breast."

Mother is irritated. She strides about and ponders. She says, "The archeological writings on this are not clear. Did it please Champoiseau's fancy to write falsely in his report that *he* found the first fragment and it was her breast?"

"Yes," insists Photi.

"No," insists the *acteur*.

She is vexed. "An impossible point of contention," she says. "How to decide? Flip a coin, franc or drachma? Is the fragment her . . . ?"

"Breast," proclaims Champoiseau.

"Wing," insists Photi. "Our grandfathers were there and saw it."

"And is the discoverer . . . ?"

"French," proclaims Champoiseau.

"Greek," insists Photi.

"Settle it," decrees Susanna. "Arm-wrestle, throw javelins. If Champoiseau wins, he uncovered it, and Photi will part for an hour with his beloved fragment."

Photi does not arm-wrestle or throw. He proposes a bicycle race.

Champoiseau assesses him coolly and asks, "Where?"

"Fengari."

We gasp.

"And back," adds Photi.

Again we gasp. Is Photi sane? Bike the summit? Never has he biked the summit. Wild goats and wasps attack there, the cold wind bites, the rocks and ridges are slick with snow. He will perish. Verily.

Photi does not flinch. "Fengari," he persists.

The *acteur* does not flinch. Showily, he welcomes this grand prix of the Aegean. "Oh, Susanna," he mimics, "what great things are done when men and mountain meet."

Susanna ignores the *acteur*. She has Photi's hand. She is taking him to the mountain.

$$6$$

*F*EARSOME MOUNT FENGARI. Crown of the Aegean.

It is a windy late afternoon of racing clouds and bending trees.

We gather where the trail begins toward the bleak,

snowy summit. We await the duel. No wagers are made. Who would bet on Photi?

He comes pedaling on his bike, in his sanctuary shirt and trousers. He entrusts his cap to Susanna, who hangs it from a tree branch. On go the goggles. For the face-punishing winds on the wild spin down.

Champoiseau arrives on foot, and because the prestige of France is on the line, he will race in consul coat and vest. From the spectators he selects a bike — any one will do — and goggles.

He pockets his gold cufflinks and folds back his sleeves. He clamps tight his pantaloons, seats himself, grasps his handlebars elitely, and preens.

Photi simply sits.

The baker spills cornstarch to designate a finish line.

Susanna shouts, "Ready!"

"Ready," answers Photi.

"Whenever," answers Champoiseau.

Susanna squeezes Photi's bell — dring-dring — and commands, "Go!"

They are off! Into the dying light, up the unpaved woodsy trail.

Photi seizes the lead. Champoiseau seizes the day; he

enjoys the ride, the foliage, the wind at his back. The trail
steepens, twists, becomes rocky. We have them in binoculars, two upended rear ends. Photi's knees are pistons; he
steers around rocks, ducks tree branches, veers along ridges.
He huffs.

Champoiseau, not huffing, seems to adhere to some
proven high style of cycling. He races as if to make a mock-
ery of it.

Up the slope they go. The burdens of Photi's life, we
feel, are riding with him like saddle packs. He pumps,
his huffs redouble . . . he maintains his lead, extends his
lead.

Binoculars find them no longer. Can Photi hold? Can
Photi, on a Thursday, elude Inevitability and wild goats and
expunge for once in his life the hex of Defeat — and win?
Win? Photi, win?

An hour passes. Twilight deepens, dapples the trail. We
watch the summit. We urge, Tcheek-tcheek tcheek-tcheek,
but little is our hope. The grind is grueling and Photi is
Photi.

The silence worries us. We hear no tires, no spokes
singing. Have the two come to a cliff and sailed off? Has
Champoiseau stopped to view Troy? pick out the lights

of Mount Athos? pack snowballs? Have wild goats attacked Photi? From a high rock did they pounce on him,
kick him?

Dring-dring, we hear at last, dring-dring. Photi emerges.
Our binoculars have him. Hurtling downward. His goggles
smeared by dust and snow, his chin blue. He is shivering, he
is soaked with perspiration; the cold wind elongates his hair.
He swerves this way, that way, lacking ballast, losing control, regaining control ... his fenders are dented, goat-
kicked, his trouser legs ripped, goat-chewed.

Champoiseau emerges, sailing, twenty yards behind. He
is unperspiring, his goggles clear. His body is an arrow flat
to gravity, and under his arm like laundry he carries a wild
baby goat. Ballast!

Champoiseau gains velocity. He and the bike and the
goat slice through the air!

Photi is anything but an arrow. His wheels swerve this
way, that way.

Our binoculars go down now. We see too well the sorry
scene.

Champoiseau's spokes are singing, seven yards behind,
six, five. Champoiseau and baby goat, noses to nose with
Photi.

Champoiseau grins. Photi grimaces.

Champoiseau waves *au revoir*.

Champoiseau's lead lengthens, six yards, nine, fifteen —
a runaway!

Champoiseau's wheels part the cornstarch. He releases
the goat and flings his hands high, a disgusting Victory sign.

Photi, without thrust, crosses the cornstarch. He
slumps over his handlebars. We rush to Photi. His face is
white, even to his lips. He pants for air. He peels off his
goggles. His woeful eyes see us but do not want to see us.
With killing literalness he utters, *"Hasame."* We lost.

A few feet beyond, Champoiseau's arms-up celebration of victory is up no longer. It collapses. And so does
Champoiseau.

AT OUR INFIRMARY, the *acteur* inhales oxygen; a cardio-
gram shows anomalies. No strenuous acting for a long time.
Off to France he must go for recuperation.

He protests, but Susanna repossesses his costume, item by item. Off come Champoiseau's shoes, vest, shirt, cuff-links, trousers. He may keep the silk underwear, but not the handkerchief. A minion collects the items from her and takes them to her room.

At dockside we give the *acteur* a sendoff. Although Champoiseau leaving Samothrace empty-handed and in jogging togs is not a sad sight, we present him a pot of hyacinths to make it even happier.

⚓ ⚓

At her table under an acacia tree, Susanna, in white blouse and mauve skirt, sips an ouzo and contemplates the script. She is wearing her hat. When she sees Photi on his bike, toting his marble under his arm, she smiles, and her foot starts to tap-tap.

Honor bound, he brakes in front of Susanna and ex-tends the marble. She accepts this, her due, and places it on the table.

We commend Photi for relinquishing the marble. He upholds the Anthropotian principle of losing gracefully, and his mother, for whom rectitude and more rectitude were what she prayed for most for him, would, if this soul-forgiven woman were still among us, highly reward him. Except by the word *highly*, we do not describe the nature of this reward, which we, all up and down our shores, are embarrassed to remember. Photi's reward, received from his mother when she was especially pleased with him, was this: to lace up her corset, on a day she chose to wear one. How do we know? We know because of the old goat, a neighbor's. It had attacked her and kicked her. How valiantly Photi smacked the goat, chased it off, told it never to return. The reward this heroism earned him was witnessed by a reliable passerby who happened to look in the window of Mrs. Anthropotis's bedroom. *There* she was, and *there* Photi was, confronting her considerable contours and — push pull — doing up her laces.

Photi stands with his back to us. Even to Susanna. How to allay the pain he feels? Our commiserations do little, so we give him news, learned in the tavernas from the film crew: the *acteur* is a professional cyclist.

Photi is hit low. He turns to Susanna. "This was known to you?" he asks.

She nods.

He is silent. Nothing of him moves for a minute, and

then he walks to his bicycle and rides away in the darkness.

Susanna rises, picks up the marble, and follows Photi down the road.

He reaches home. He walks past his bird feeder and into his small white house. She arrives. She taps on his door, but he does not open it. She knocks.

He does not open.

She knocks insistently.

The door opens partway and Photi stands there, miffed. He glares at her.

"Kyrie Photi," she says, "I was thinking of the script. The poetry, the power of the breast. I put that first. I should not have. I am sorry."

He opens the door a little wider.

She offers the marble.

He does not move to accept it. He is nobly hurt.

"I will film with the widow's doorstop," she says. "It will do."

She offers the marble again.

He does not reach for it.

"Take it," she demands impatiently. "Forgive Mother with a kiss and take it."

Photi accepts the marble. She offers her cheek.

He will not kiss her. He closes the door — almost; her foot is quick.

She pushes inside. She hurls her hat to the floor. She is agitated, angry. He is startled. She slaps his face. A wicked slap, it bends him. He is frightened. He clutches the marble.

She stands over him, scowling. "Mule," she denounces.

He cringes. He collapses on the carpet, hugging the marble. He lies motionless with it.

"Crawl," she commands.

He begins to crawl on his knees and elbows with the marble. She follows. Her foot goads him. "Haul your cunt-cult marble," she barks. "Place her on her throne."

He crawls to the bedroom. Without rising, he places the marble on the nightstand beside his mother's photograph.

"Kiss her," she commands. "It's a saint's day."

He kisses the marble. Humiliated, he slumps on the floor.

She stands over him, legs wide. "Look up," she commands.

He looks up her skirt. She is alfresco.

He cannot stop gazing up her mauve skirt.

"I do not think you like it," she derides. "Do not like it at all."

He does. He could look up her skirt for a long time.

"Wells dry up. Floods, droughts, and avalanches afflict the world. But isn't a frizzy auburn cunt the nicest plague of all?"

He says nothing. His gaze up her legs is intent.

"So, you won't be bothered with it?"

His shoulders respond, rise, and his head maneuvers up inside her skirt. "Not be bothered with it at all," she berates, and his head moves farther up.

"It's not caring enough, is what it probably is," she complains, which brings his chin up farther, just where Mother wants it to be.

"A peck," she pouts, and awaits better. Better received, she expects better yet and lifts her skirt to witness his obeisance. Better yet received, she commands, "Up, mule."

He stands, face flushed with the ecstasy of abasement.

"Do you know you upset me?" she scolds. "Upset me terribly?" He nods ashamedly. "Are you or are you not my love? My very special love?"

Trembling, near tears, he murmurs, "Yes, Mother."

"Wretched boy. Went to Paris and fucked that hussy. Didn't you?"

He is silent, then starts to weep. He comes to her, wanting to be embraced.

Mother is not done with him, not done with him at all. "What must Mother do?" she frets.

He is trembling. He is silent.

"You know what Mother must do."

He unbuckles his leather belt.

She removes her blouse for the meting out to be done. She whips the belt from his trousers. She brandishes it. He removes his trousers and shorts; he cups his genitals; he arches belly down at the bedside.

"I do not think you like it," she laments, "do not like it at all." And, leather whistling, she opens on him.

~ 8 ~

UNDER THE ACACIA TREE, Susanna's cameraman and propman sit with her. They have been through actor crises before. They have solved Cellini, Turner, Rodin.

Susanna, hatless, wears a long white summer dress with gathers. It has a mauve Hapsburg collar. Always on Susanna, something mauve.

The propman, a sturdy sort in short pants, hum-sings, "I looked over Jordan and what did I see, coming for to take me to Pa-ree? A band of angels . . ."

The band of angels is us. We come by to express our regrets. How can Susanna's filming proceed without Champoiseau?

"With a new Champoiseau," she replies.

Where to find a Frenchman? we ask.

"A Samothracian will do," she says. "A brave one, one who would kiss a she-wolf or run off with your goddess."

To France? we ask.

"To Samothrace," she replies.

The words go to our spines. To Samothrace?

She repeats, "To Samothrace."

Mouths open, we intone: To Samothrace.

She rises and assesses us. We are lesser varieties of the person she needs. She walks to the sanctuary.

Photi stands alone at the findspot. She comes near. His face is solemn, red as a whip-welt. He will not look at her.

"Kyrie Photi," she says, "I believe you have my hat."

He will not talk.

"The ribbon you may keep."

He stares at the stones of the findspot.

"You like my ribbon, don't you? Its delicate pink sections?"

He says nothing. He is humiliated. Must the whole island hear of this?

Susanna sits on a rock and faces him.

"Victory, Kyrie Photi? What is Victory? An enjoyed success? A ribbon won, presented to one and not another? Is Victory the apples of the Hesperides? the fleece of gold? a bike race?"

Photi stands silent. He will listen.

"My father left Arcadia to find Victory in the snows of Wisconsin. He, too, idealized Victory. America! America! In Victory we trust. Winning isn't everything, it's the only thing. What happened was marriage, a chain of restaurants, and me."

Turning a little sideways to her, Photi asks, "Was that not something?"

"Bankruptcy and abandonment," she replies. "My mother splits. I never saw her again. Daddy raises me — if by 'raises' we mean far-off private schools and college, and if by 'Daddy' we mean a man to whom I'm baggage. I crimp his philandering style. Daddy, you see, is Daddy-o to bustful redheads and blondes. I graduate, take up with a Turk, a broker of stolen jewels worldwide — an Ottoman oppressor who makes me feel coddled and kept. He kept beating me, you see, and kept a harem. And I kept loving him until I didn't. Daddy forgive? Never. I scoot. I live a stone-rolling — or rolling-stone — life, making documentaries about art."

Sadly, she says, "A rolling stone, Kyrie Photi, gathers no remorse."

Photi knows a stone aphorism or two himself, including one from Seferis, but he does not quote it.

"Bingo," says Susanna. "Daddy wins three million do-la-ri-a in the state lottery. Leaves me zero. He does what my mother did, abandons me. Wills everything to three harlots — one who dyed his hair, one who pedicured his toes, and one who cured everything else. He couldn't express the sorrow he felt for his own life. All the flutes in Arcadia couldn't. He dies in his Cadillac, buried in a snowdrift. Victory . . . ?"

Photi is saddened. He moves toward her. He wants to comfort her.

She makes space for him on the rock. He sits.

"Ah, Susanna," he says, "sometimes we think we are being delivered to the grinning animals, but we must keep to something, a faith, a statue, a beautiful woman . . . and her ribbon."

"Kyrie Photi," she replies, "life is one grand buoyed-up romance with Victory. The wings of Victory are cheap soulbird symbolism. Your Nike is faceless, a pseudo–mother angel, her roots everywhere and nowhere. And we, what are we? Her orphans, flotsam on the waters."

Photi demurs. He speaks softly, patiently. "Victory there is, Susanna. Without her, we are a procession of the living dead. She is our flower, our soul. The great Welsh poet Dylan Thomas wrote, 'The force that through the green fuse drives the flower drives my green age.' That is Victory, Susanna: fuse and flower . . . humanity."

Susanna has whipped him; now she endures him. She listens.

"Even in tragedy, triumph. Blind Oedipus at Colonus, dying at a great age in full, rich serenity. Hamlet sung to his rest by angels. The moving shadows the chained man sees on the wall of Plato's cave. Those shadows are wings, Susanna, wings of Victory. She is there, Susanna, even in a snowdrift."

He rises. He has talked too much. He was told by his mother not to talk too much.

She smiles sadly. "Ah, wings of Victory." She sighs. "Is there a flight of spiritual thought that has not had its echo in Greek literature?"

Photi feels compassion. He takes her hand and she stands facing him.

"For you, Susanna," he asks, "would not something be Victory? What is that something?"

She comes closer to him. "Something, yes, would be Victory," she replies. "To document a miracle."

Photi loves miracles. Fish and flowers are miracles,

birds too, even some free verse. But he is sorry. He cannot understand.

"A miracle?" he says.

"The Victory of Victory herself." She pauses. "Do you follow me?"

He shakes his head.

"Kyrie Photi, Victory for me would be to bring to the screen some astounding event as it happens, as it becomes a miracle, and gives an ordinary mortal a place, a niche in immortality . . . just as burial in a royal tomb does."

"Ah, say more," pleads Photi.

Point blank, she declares, "Repatriation."

The noun swallows the air. Photi loses his breath for a moment.

"Repatriation," she repeats, "as it actually happens. The lost daughter brought gloriously home . . . to her family . . . to wildly cheering Samothracians — who go absolutely bonkers."

Bonkers? The expression excites Photi. He hears trumpets in it, wild clarinets.

"Do you follow me now?" she asks, and he nods vigorously.

She goes on: "The Nike repatriated, reenshrined. Her

glorious fountain rebuilt, the streamlets feeding again, the freshening waters curling and bubbling over the pebbles."

"Yes, yes," exclaims Photi, "I follow. My mind is a sky-of-blue canvas, and on it I see nothing else."

"Kyrie Photi," she says, "you and I are going to make a documentary *and* history. I have a new ending for this script. A new title: 'Repatriation.' *Epanapatrismos.*"

Photi shivers. This woman has spoken the Word, can even pronounce it correctly.

"Monsieur Photi," she proclaims, "you are going to wear the French pantaloons, vest, and gold cufflinks and be my Champoiseau."

Photi emits a scoffing laugh. "Champoiseau? My skin breaks out thinking of him."

"Makeup, cosmetics, don't you see? Under the costume you are Photi Anthropotis, pride of the bunch here, come to Paris on a mission, like an Argonaut. Your mission: bring the pussy home."

"Do you seek to make a fool of me?" he asks. "Poetry finds room in my head when you talk, Susanna, but me Champoiseau? Impossible. I am Photi. No antiquarian, no —"

Susanna's fingers go to his lips. She completes his sentence: "Frenchman."

Photi is flustered.

"Monsieur Photi, if Champoiseau can shout Eureka like a Greek, you can walk like a Frenchman and talk English like a Frenchman."

Photi walks to the findspot. He gets down on one knee and removes his cap. He is either praying or taking an oath, or maybe just tying his shoelaces.

Susanna goes to Photi's side. "Monsieur Photi, how else can you repatriate?"

His eyes rise to hers. *"Americana,"* he asks, "what is in this for you?"

"A director's dream," she replies. "A documentary that documents an astounding, miraculous act. Repatriation. Epic event, as it happens. It will win acclaim, awards."

"Like *Never on Sunday*?" he asks.

"Like *Never on Sunday*."

He rises and puts on his cap. He feels befuddled. "How will I, as Champoiseau, repatriate our Nike?"

"The script," says Susanna, "the script. It's the play — wherein we catch the conscience of *le musée.* It is 1909. Champoiseau is seventy-nine and near death."

"Seventy-nine?" Photi is dismayed.

"You will look it, Kyrie Photi. The play of light, a little makeup."

"Only a play of light and a little makeup," laments Photi, "and I look near death and French?"

"The commemoration scene," Susanna heralds with a flourish of her arms. "Champoiseau — you — is brought to the Louvre in a wheelchair. A ramp is put down for the chair — to ascend the stairs. The mayor and other dignitaries are there to honor you. A band plays the national anthem. The mayor pins a medal on you, exalts you as a gallant son of France whose contribution to her glory will be sung for centuries. You nod agreement."

Photi shakes his head. No, he will not nod. He doubts very much his capacity to ever, ever nod agreement.

"Hate yourself," she says, "but nod agreement. Just a tiny little French nod, that's all."

Photi shakes his head again.

"Kyrie Photi, you can do it. A tiny tip downward of the head and — fait accompli — you have nodded, you have acknowledged the achievement of Champoiseau."

Photi is doubtful, but listens.

"The mayor praises you to the heights. You and your Victory are up there with Marie Curie, Joan of Arc. But, alas, you are dying. What good are accolades? You want ascension — to be borne to heaven on the wings of your Nike."

Photi understands ascension. Forget plucked out of the sea by helicopter. Ascension. Borne to heaven.

"Kyrie Photi, are you light on your feet?"

"D'Artagnan," assures Photi.

Hardly convinced, she continues: "During the eulogies, you lurch forward and grasp the edge of the stone prow. You address the Nike, '*Ah, ma Victoire*, I am dying. I brought you up from the dead. Now up from the dead you will bring me.' Amazingly, you leap like a balletist, grab the ledge, and hoist yourself onto the prow. You sit there, gathering breath. The audience is aghast. A guard rushes to stop you."

"The guard, a woman?"

"Women weren't guards in 1909," says Susanna, "but for your Parisian *petite amie* we take poetic license."

"Gabrielle does not recognize me?"

"She does not recognize you."

"Your cosmetics disguise me. I am a dying old man."

"You rise to your feet. You embrace the legs of the statue. You shimmy up her torso. You perch there — between the wings. You feel incomparable bliss. You stand and thrust your arms skyward. You yourself are Victory! You yourself have wings."

"Do I fall and break my neck?"

"You stand there and recite to the sky what the great Kazantzakis put on his stone in Crete: 'I hope for nothing. I fear nothing. I am free.'"

"But Kazantzakis" — Photi does the arithmetic on his fingers — "was twenty-four in 1909."

"Poetic liberty," says Susanna. "Enjoy it. You are Greek."

Photi enjoys it very much, but he must ask, "How will I come down?"

"You do not come down."

"I fly to Parnassus like Bellerophon?"

"The scene ends there. An apotheosis. The Nike of Samothrace and Champoiseau, astride her wings. One icon, one spirit."

Photi laughs regretfully. "Ah, Susanna, impossible. *Le Musée du Louvre* let an actor climb atop our Nike? Never."

"The *dummy*, Kyrie Photi, the replica," she replies. "The Louvre has granted us permission to shoot at night and bring the island's copy Nike up the Daru stairs for the two scenes we have to do there."

Photi's eyes enlarge. "The second scene?"

"The finale," she says. "A true-to-history scene. It is 1939. The Nike is brought down the Daru stairs on a plank, before the Nazi vultures enter Paris. She is spirited away to a hideout in the south of France."

"An escape scene," says Photi, excitement elevating him another inch.

"Escape from the Nazis — ostensibly."

"Ostensibly," repeats Photi, pleased by the word. "The Louvre will allow os-ten-si-bly?"

Susanna takes his hand and leads him down the path to our small museum. It is a quiet room. They are alone.

The headless replica Nike stands like a scandalous relative in a corner. She has the full height of the genuine Nike but no prow to stand on.

"Touch her, Kyrie Photi."

He touches her hem.

"What do you feel?"

"Plaster of Paris."

"Heavy-duty," she says. "She will hold."

"Hold?"

"You."

"Me?"

"Fortunately, avoirdupois-wise, you are more of a leprechaun than a Hercules."

Photi is puzzled. "Go on."

Susanna goes on: "To dramatize the victory of France over the Nazi looters, the Louvre will allow my cameras to shoot the *faux* Nike coming down ... down ... the stairs ..."

The *down ... down* excites Photi. He repeats each *down, down.*

"... and into a van," she says.

"A van?"

"French cavalry. The kind horses go to war in."

Excitedly he says, "Down the stairs ... and into a van ... the kind horses go to war in."

She singsongs, "The *faux* Nike ... descends ... the stairs," and the words have such poetry, Photi singsongs them too.

How deliciously *faux* is the word *faux!*

Photi is floating now. He singsongs, "The *faux* Nike not coming down the stairs will be ... the real Nike coming down the stairs."

"*Oui,*" says Mother Susanna.

Photi's knuckles knock happily on the dummy. "This plaster saint will be repatriated to France," he singsongs.

Susanna, in singsong, completes the perfidy. "And the real Nike will be repatriated to Samothrace."

Photi is nearly ecstatic. "But how?" he asks. "How?"

"The French have a word: *legerdemain*."

"Trickery, deceit," says Photi, words suddenly sacrosanct.

"Sleight of hand," Susanna prefers.

"Now you see her," says Photi, "now you don't."

"Fake or real, in movies it's the play of lights."

Photi assesses the fake Nike. "She has her pallor," he admits. "She has hips, wings . . ." Still, he is doubtful. "One glance and even a blind guard would smell her and shout Pretender."

"A blind guard, perhaps," says Susanna, "but a woman in love with you?"

Photi laughs to dismiss such a thought, then asks, "Do you think so?"

"Monsieur Photi, I think so."

Photi grins. He knows the milk of opportunism when he gets a sip of it. But sweet as it is, a pact must be sealed. He places his hand on the dummy. Susanna covers his hand with hers. Pact sealed, he withdraws his hand. He has re-membered something. "I do not drive."

Just looking at him, Susanna knows that. "Your driver will be my propman. He has a map and is studying the roads out of Paris. He will drive the van to an out-of-the-way dock in Italy. There, a speedy clipper ship, Greek flag flying, will await you and Her Marble Majesty."

Photi is now ecstatic. He gives tune to "And . . . we . . . come . . . sail-ing . . . sail-ing home."

"Can you pilot a clipper?" she asks.

"Caïque or clipper, no difference."

Susanna turns to the replica Nike. "Cunt, be good and you'll sleep the night in the Louvre with the Mona and the Milo. While Mama and her crew hightail it back here to shoot the grand finale. Sam-o-thra-kee will go bonkers, ab-so-lute-ly bonkers!"

Photi sings out rapturously, "Go bonkers, ab-so-lute-ly bonkers."

He must venerate. He drops to his knees and seizes Susanna. His arms encircle her waist. He squeezes her. His face presses into her long white dress — at the gathers, where, if she were sitting, her laptop would be.

Her fingers caress his ears. Softly, she speaks to him, as if poking food to a bird: "Nowhere, ever, a repatriation so glorious. Nowhere a hero so true to the part. Photi Anthropotis and his Nike arriving home on the clipper, Greek flag hoisted, ship horn sounding. Dot-dot-dot-dash, dot-dot-dot-dash. Jubilation! Cheers! Bravo! *Yasoo!* Church bells clamoring, flags flurrying, hundreds of flags flurrying in dizzy ecstasy. France shocked, the world amazed, all Hellas euphoric."

She stops. He is trembling. His face presses in at her Venus point.

"Kyrie Photi, can you do it?"

He is crying. He cannot speak. He remains on his knees. She is his orchid and, there where she is most orchidaceous, his face is lost in her.

"Kyrie Photi, can you do it?" she demands with a rising inflection. "Can you? Can you bring pussy home?"

He looks up at her. Tears have swallowed his eyes. He says nothing, but Mother knows. Kyrie Photi can do it. He can bring pussy home.

She pats his head. "You have my hat, Kyrie Photi. Bring it up tonight. Mother will dress you as Champoiseau."

9

WE CROWD THE SANCTUARY the next day to witness the discovery. The bare-chested diggers stand circled at the findspot. They await Susanna and her new Champoiseau.

Down the road they come, Mother, Photi, and marble. Photi wears Champoiseau's shoes, shirt, vest, pantaloons, and gold cufflinks. Costume seen to by Mother. Shirt tucked in by Mother, vest buttoned and hair combed by Mother, without so much from him as a "You embarrass me," we would wager. On these trousers there is no button missing.

Mother today is in mauve leotards and white blouse. She wears her wide hat, still pinkly beribboned. That's Photi, we jest: accept no substitute!

He carries his marble at a slow I'm-condemned-to-be-sunk pace. At the findspot he presents the marble to

Susanna. It's a ceremony, like some ancient changing of the matriarchate guard. Susanna accepts the marble with solemnity and turns it over to the propman.

"Bury this tit," she directs him. And off to mock burial goes Mrs. Anthropotis.

Photi walks to a rise and stands there, looking down on Champoiseau's hired Greeks with shovels.

Susanna orders silence.

Actors in place, cameras ready, the action begins.

CHAMPOISEAU: There the Austrians failed. Here the French, time-honored friends of Greece, will succeed. (*He turns to the diggers.*) Homeric men of Samothrace, let the gods hear your shovels, for the glory of Greece.

The digging starts.

FIRST DIGGER: What lip we endure in the name of the glory of Greece.

SECOND DIGGER: Amateur antiquarians wear fancy shoes.

THIRD DIGGER: The Frenchman pays in francs.

FOURTH DIGGER: *Doxa patris.* Glory to our country.

ALL DIGGERS (*resignedly*): *Doxa patris. Doxa patris.*

CHAMPOISEAU: *Doxa patris.*

"Cut!" demands Susanna. "Sly-ly, Monsieur Champoiseau, you must speak the line sly-ly. You are a Frenchman."

Photi, in three takes, finally utters *"Doxa patris"* slyly.

The digging continues as the narrator (Susanna) reads:

Our grandfathers saw the Frenchman with the fancy shoes. They were paid by him to dig. They felt the excitement of discovery. They heard the cries of exultation.

Champoiseau, wielding his shovel, strikes a hard object. He digs and wrests from the ground a round marble fragment. He clutches it.

CHAMPOISEAU (*shouting excitedly*): Eureka! Eureka!

The diggers run to crowd around Champoiseau. He clutches the marble passionately to his chest.

CHAMPOISEAU (*shouting*): A breast! A breast!

ALL DIGGERS: Our Nike! Our Nike!

CHAMPOISEAU (*possessively*): Our Nike! Our Nike!

"Cut!" orders Susanna. "Champoiseau, the script must be read as written: Champoiseau pos-ses-sive-ly exclaims, 'My Nike! My Nike!'"

Photi winces.

"And you must clutch the beloved marble pas-sion-ate-ly to your chest. Pas-sion-ate-ly."

Photi blushes like a little red lamp.

On the retake he complies.

CHAMPOISEAU (*clutches the fragment pas-sion-ate-ly to his chest and pos-ses-sive-ly exclaims*): My Nike! My Nike!

The diggers look at each other, perplexed.

CHAMPOISEAU (*still clutching the marble to his chest*): Mitera! Mitera!

"Cut!" Susanna pleads with Photi: "*Mère! Mère!* You are French, Champoiseau. The feelings of France are your feelings."

Photi grimaces, and on the retake almost chokes, but he utters it: *Mère! Mère!*

ALL DIGGERS (*in awe and in chorus*): Mitera! Mitera!

CHAMPOISEAU (*runs happily down the road shouting*): Eureka! Eureka! *Mitera! Mitera!*

"Cut! Champoiseau, you must run hap-pi-ly down the road. Hap-pi-ly. And shout *Mère! Mère!* Not *Mitera! Mitera!*"

On the third retake, Champoiseau runs hap-pi-ly down the road.

In three more takes, he is able to shout an acceptably French *Mère! Mère!* as he runs hap-pi-ly down the road.

End of scene.

"Monsieur Photi," exclaims Susanna, "you are so French and wonderful! Now we box the dummy, and off we go to Paris."

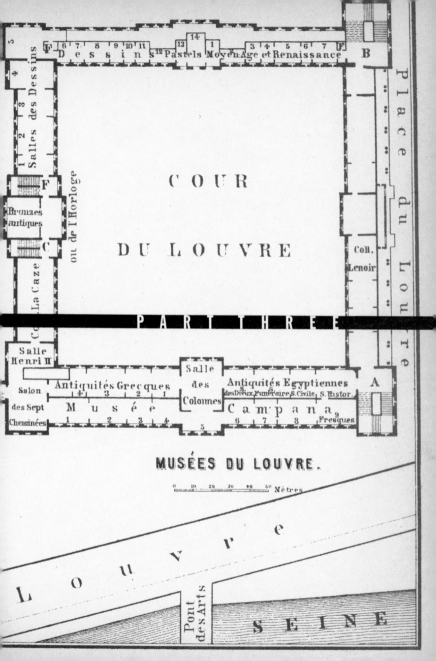

PART THREE

MUSÉES DU LOUVRE.

⇜ 1 ⇝

ONLY A FEW DAYS have Photi, Susanna, and her film crew been gone, but already our necks turn to watch for the two-a-day boat.

Today the boat brings us two surprises. Photi's father, overweight and overbearing in a wide-lapeled American suit. The second surprise: he is alone.

"Divorce," Pindaros Anthropotis explains to us. "A favorite pastime in Ah-mer-ica."

We commiserate with Pindaros. Such are the ways of marriage in the New World. Better it would have been not to elope to Ah-mer-ica but to marry in the church and stick like a thistle to the soil you were born in. You would still have your job at the sanctuary. You would have your house.

"Where is pebblehead?" demands Pindaros.

Paris, we reply.

"To receive the Nobel Prize for poetry?"

Photi acts in a movie, we tell him.

"Acts!" Pindaros scoffs. "He is impotent."

He acts the part of Champoiseau, we tell him.

Pindaros absorbs this news slowly. He holds his head in amazement. "A Greek? Play Champoiseau?"

She begged him to play the part, we say.

"She?"

The *Americana*. PBS. She has inspired him. He will bring back our Nike.

Pindaros laughs. "Riding on marble wings, my son will fly back shouting *E-pan-a-pa-tris-mos?* It is good he has another job, because I return to the sanctuary."

With dismay we contemplate this declaration. We know what an island-wide ventilation of opinion will ensue from it. Pindaros or Photi? To whom belongs the safe-keeping of the Sanctuary of the Great Gods?

Before we sleep tonight, we will pray that Photi someday will be less a weight on his father.

We remember the tribulations Pindaros bore, trying to find his way as a widower, suffering a son who wrote poetry

and slept in the sanctuary, a son who believed, without saying so, that his father had dishonored the memory of his
wife by handing down the basket in church so he could dis-
play his mourning armband and look our women over one
by one.

Where will you live? we ask.

"Has this island gone bananas?" shouts Pindaros. "The
house of Pindaros Anthropotis is the house of Pindaros
Anthropotis until the stonecutter cuts the name in stone."

We sigh profoundly for Photi. No job, no house, no
mother, no wife. No poem in the paper. Only our Nike in
the Louvre has he now to hold to.

WITHOUT PHOTI FOR A WEEK, we watch the horizon for
him. When the candles we light melt away, we light longer
ones. We watch the news. No bulletins from Paris, no
shouts of French indignation: *Scandale! Scandale!* No premier

addresses a distressed nation, promising capture, justice, vowing that *honneur* must be restored in the name of France. What we see on the news is hunger in Africa, bank robberies, weather reports.

In new blue shirt and cap, Pindaros Anthropotis has re-installed himself at the sanctuary. He walks alone among the ruins, kicking the stones. "I am back. I have repatri-ated." He laughs callously.

At the findspot, he raises his arms and scoffs, "Speak, stones, move! Rise, become a fountain! Purify sinners!" He laughs. "In Ah-mer-ica they say, 'Ivory soap, ninety-nine and forty-four hundredths percent pure. It floats.'"

A BOAT APPEARS ON THE CURVE. We watch it turn and commit to our harbor. It docks. Susanna and her film crew. No Photi! No Photi! They have the look of a vanguard that has tasted victory.

Under her wide beribboned hat, Susanna stands on the deck, a dame mother with her cameras. A song is going on inside her head. She disembarks. We crowd around her. She awaits our silence. Coolly she says, "Your Nike stands no longer in the Louvre."

We do not react. We are inured to cosmic news. Tell us Perseus has escaped the sky, tell us "Star Trek" reruns have been canceled.

"She is coming home," says Susanna. "She is on the road. In the custody of Kyrie Photi Anthropotis."

Can we believe this woman?

"I am here to shoot her return," she says, and she holds high, in the sign of Victory, two videocassettes. "Come, see."

She walks to the sanctuary. We follow.

On the stone wall of the fountain ruins, her crew in short pants sets up a television and a video player.

We gather around, a human amphitheater. Photi's father stands with us, disbelieving.

"Cassette one," she announces. "The Champoiseau commemoration scene. Shot at night. The Louvre closed."

She presses the Play button. This is what we see:

Our Photi as Champoiseau, in a wheelchair. In the

Louvre! Our Photi, who is always half out of pictures we have of him, is now in full-screen color before us. His hair powdered gray, his skin professionally wrinkled, he is an antiquated antiquarian, splendidly garbed in a fine vested suit, with gold cufflinks, and recognizable as Photi only by us, who prayed each night for him.

He maneuvers the wheelchair down the long Hall of Antiquities and stops at the bottom of the Daru stairs. He looks up to the flag- and flower-bedecked landing.

The costumed mayor and other dignitaries, seated there to honor him, rise and applaud his arrival.

The statue stands on her prow.

"Do you recognize her?" asks Susanna.

Yes, we moan, we would know that cheap impostor anywhere.

"The gen-u-ine Nike," she says in a voice hushed, as befits such a mystical achievement, "stands off in a corner, under a shroud, out of camera range."

We watch Susanna's piano movers place a plank over the stairs, and then we see proud Photi, seventy-nine, being slowly wheeled up the plank by a sturdy female Louvre guard.

Gabrielle? we ask.

Susanna nods.

As Champoiseau and Gabrielle ascend to the landing, a band plays "La Marseillaise." All are standing except Champoiseau.

"See his tears?" asks Susanna, and yes, in Photi's face, in close-up now, we see tears — bogus tears for a bogus Nike. Or is it his allergy amid the ceremonial flowers?

Photi maneuvers his chair away from the flowers, toward the base of the statue, the prow.

The band plays the Greek national anthem, "Hymn to Liberty." All remain standing. Photi remains seated — with the glue of superhuman strength, he remains seated.

The dignitaries eulogize Champoiseau and his discovery. A medal is pinned on him. Photi subdues a grimace, but he is moved. French flattery, irresistible. Any flattery is irresistible to our Photi. He nods agreement without difficulty. Enjoys it so much he nods a second time! Now he grasps the edge of the prow and looks up to the wings of his Nike. He addresses her:

"*Ma Victoire,* I am dying. I brought you up from the dead — dead but still breathing. Now up from the dead you will bring me — still breathing but dead."

Dramatically, he rises. He pumps his arms and up he

springs. Like a superannuated Nijinsky he bounds — and plops down with a bump of his rear on the prow. We have seen Photi hop the stones of the sanctuary, seen him bike our rocky slopes with no hands, do somersaults in his slingchair, but this?

The guard hurries toward him.

Writhing, twisting, he moves up the legs of the statue. He encircles her waist, and his head finds a niche between her breasts.

Our Photi, we cry. Up on the Nike! Never mind that she is fake, and the guard knows it; never mind that Photi is playing Champoiseau, and the guard does not know it. Photi is the star. He is up on the Nike! Plaster of Paris! Tears wet our faces.

"Come down, Monsieur Champoiseau," pleads Gabrielle.

Disengage himself? Never. "I am Champoiseau," he declares, "the Columbus of the art world. Savior of Victory."

Unthwarted by gravity, he springs — half somersault, half jiggle — and up he goes, landing like a kinetic miracle of protoplasm between her wings.

We shield our eyes. The statue will crack, we cry. Photi will die. We want never to see our Photi plunge and die broken-boned, even as Champoiseau.

Photi's father coldly watches.

Gabrielle pleads, "Please, Monsieur Champoiseau, come to me."

He ignores her. He wants to be borne to heaven on the wings of his Nike. The bliss of impending ascension is helium inside him.

A ladder is brought. The guard climbs onto the prow. As if to a cat, she cajoles, "Come down, Monsieur Champoiseau, come down."

Down? Down is no direction for Champoiseau. He rises to his feet, standing upright on the statue's neck. He is noble humanity, aimed like the barrel of a pistol to be shot through the skylight.

He speaks. Beyond the skylight, high into the Pantocratic night, our Photi recites the Kazantzakis epitaph: "I hope for nothing. I fear nothing. I am free."

He remains upright, arms upraised. There is a moment of holy silence. The screen whitens.

We have witnessed. We are awed. We cry, Bravo, Photi, bravo!

The white screen persists, its whiteness like the promised hue of heaven. Photi has risen, we cry, Photi has risen! Verily!

We applaud. We cry, Bravo, Susanna! May you win laurels.

Photi's father, dumbfounded, says nothing.

Susanna inserts the second cassette.

It was shot the same night. The scene: thirty years later, 1939, the Nazis approach Paris. She presses Play.

We see the Nike, upright in a shroud, her figure clasped by the hands of sturdy piano movers. The plank that brought Champoiseau up will now bring the Nike down.

Our Nike? Which Nike? *Faux* or real?

We see the prow on the landing. The Nike on the prow — is she the dummy? Oh, Susanna, say it — she *is* the dummy!

Susanna smiles the canary smile.

Ah, the stratagem! We see. Wonderful *legerdemain*.

Tenderly, with block and tackle, the piano movers lower our shrouded Nike. Silence alone is fitting. Our treasure, our Victory, being brought down to ground level, to be hidden from the depraved Nazis.

The screen splits, and we see the descent of the shrouded Nike on one side, and on the other, Hitler loudly ranting: "One should guard against believing the great masses to be more stupid than they are."

Out into the night comes our Nike — into the street, the fumes, and the noise of hoi polloi.

So much for nine points of the law.

A vintage cavalry van stands parked there. The rear door swings open. With a tilt at the doorway, our Nike is escorted upright into the dark cargo space — and off the stage of the world.

"Off to the races!" exclaims Susanna.

Magnificent! we chant. Unbelievable! This is true, not a movie. Susanna Regas, you are wonderful. PBS is wonderful.

Mother smiles. "Who sits in the van?" she asks, and the camera pans to the passenger window.

Photi! we proclaim. Photi!

Still disguised, there he is! Not at all risen to heaven. Our Photi. Holding a hot hand, but calm. A French medal pinned on his lapel. Miracle! we cry. Miracle! Our Nike and Photi, passengers back to back, in a van. But a driver? Who will drive?

Out of the Louvre rushes Gabrielle. She runs with a schoolgirl's abandon, her hand holding her cap in place. She reaches the van and sees Photi in the passenger seat. Now she knows him. "Yes, it's Photi!" she shrieks with amazement. "Photi! Are you crazy?"

Susanna's sturdy propman/driver is behind the van, hurriedly trying to secure the door.

"Photi," we hear Gabrielle say, "you are either a genius or a fool."

Photi is silent, on a mission. He awaits his driver.

Gabriélle leaps into the driver's seat, revs the engine. Off lurches the van, straight into the night, the startled propman/driver abandoned, stunned, immobile.

Photi unpins the medal and flips it out the window.

The screen whitens.

We cheer. We cry. *Doxa! Doxa!* Glory! Glory! Photi and his angel Gabrielle on the loose with our Nike. Photi and our Nike heading home. Across France and Italy, heading home!

"To a secret dock," says Susanna. "A clipper awaits. Photi will pilot."

"It will sink," says Photi's father.

We hush the man. Rejoice, we tell him, rejoice. No ~ Nike an effigy in the Louvre. Our Nike and ~d! They are coming home! Home!

Anthropotis.

him. We grasp each other's shoul-

t to soar with euphoria and sing, but

our legs hold back. Too soon it is to dance and sing, to un-
plug the barrels.

We run to televisions. Weather reports, cowboy movies.
Where is wing-footed Hermes with the news?

On it comes. Bulletins. The Nike of Samothrace, missing. Taken! Mysteriously stolen! The Nike of Samothrace —
island of ancient mysteries — gone! France, outraged. The
Louvre has dyspepsia. French folk everywhere declare, *Scandale! Scandale!*

The theft of the century! The deception of the century!

We crowd around Susanna and hear the TV broadcasts.

A fake Nike stands on the prow in the Louvre. A cab-
bage! The Nike *authentique, pfft!* Who is this Houdini? What
is his price?

We hear the amazing news. The Louvre opened the
next day and no one noticed that the Nike atop the stairs
was fake. No one! Even the substitute guard did not recognize that the substitute Nike was the substitute Nike.
Tourists gave their usual sighs of awe and admiration. Some
found her monotonously triumphant.

Who discovered the loss? The dusting lady. When the
Louvre closed for the night, she dusted. Plaster on her
duster!

Susanna wishes she could have documented *that* on film.

We laugh, we cry, we embrace each other. We have joined the saints in glory. Verily.

Where, demands the televised world, is the genuine Nike, the Greek genie? Who are these thieves of the night? To whom does Victory belong?

The world becomes an instantaneous Babel of debates. Bartenders across the globe are interviewed. Curators pontificate. Sotheby's and Christie's recoin the word *priceless.* The capitals of Europe fear conspiracy. The United Nations, to assure stability, will issue a measured statement. The world is becoming one contentious coffeehouse. Nimble-speaking ambassadors speak unnimbly. A gloomy-faced premier of France addresses his nation. He displays an irrational aversion to the sudden absence of our Nike. The culprits will have no peace until the pride of the Louvre — *notre Victoire de Samothrace* — is repatriated!

At her table under an acacia tree, Susanna sips ouzo and takes phone calls. One is from Photi, in Italy.

"*Buon giorno,* Mother," he says.

"Kyrie Photi!"

"Our Nike, be assured, is well. Gabrielle drives like an angel. Who can catch her? Champoiseau is with us."

"Champoiseau?" exclaims Susanna.

We hear the name. We groan.

"He sleeps at the feet of our Nike."

"I worry," says Susanna.

We, too, worry. Out come our beads. Worry is all we will do until we see our Photi on the curve, sailing home.

"Do not worry," Photi tells her. "No bike race. We will reach our destination — where is it?"

"A tiny dock above Brindisi. Vérité."

"I will find Vérité. The clipper awaits?"

"The clipper awaits, skipper."

"Caïque or clipper, no difference," Photi says, and he asks, "You have good pictures for America, or was I a hole in the screen?"

"Kyrie Photi, you are a Thespian."

"Never on Sunday?" asks Photi.

"Never on Sunday."

"The island," asks Photi, "it will go bonkers?"

"Bonkers," assures Susanna.

"Verily," says Photi, and hangs up.

We pray. In our churches, homes, tavernas, and coffee-houses, we ask: God, deliver our Photi. God, deliver our Nike.

God, we believe, will be pleased that first in our prayers we place Photi.

~ *4* ~

OUR SHUTTERS REMAIN OPEN through the night. The shutters of Photi's father's house stay latched.

Dawn comes. Tuesday. No Photi. Mother's camera crew has finale fever. Anxiously they stand watch at dockside. They do not sleep. Mother, though worried, sleeps.

Night comes, no Photi.

We light longer candles, say longer prayers.

Still shut: the shutters of the Anthropotis house.

Dawn. Wednesday. The cameras are hungry.

Through the mist, a spar. Rigging. A white clipper ... with an excited Greek flag. Eureka! Our binoculars have him. Photi at the helm, in vest and pantaloons.

E-pan-a-pa-tris-mos! we shout. The syllables come out of us like cymbal crashes. Under a shroud, on deck, our Nike, our icon. Liberated! Home!

The camera crew documents.

O God! we cry, our prayers answered. Our Nike, home! Home!

Euphoria, ecstasy, jubilation. We cheer wildly. Our arms fling skyward. Nike! Nike! Home! Home!

Susanna arrives and solemnly watches the clipper grow larger as it approaches. She seems not to hear our celebration. She listens for a horn. Three dots, a dash.

Joyfully, tearfully, we wave flags, our arms, our shirts. Church bells announce the coming. Nike! Nike! Oh, the wonderful luck, to live in the Age of the Return of Our Nike!

Photi's father opens his shutters halfway.

The clipper moves near. There are no three dots and a dash yet, but surely Photi is aboard with our Nike. There will be three dots and a dash, we pray . . . there will be.

Bravo, Photi! we cry. *Yasoo!* Our beloved Photi home! Our beloved Nike home! Repatriation! *E-pan-a-pa-tris-mos!*

We sing the soul-lifting verses of our national anthem, shivering with anticipation.

The clipper touches dock. Without dots, without dash. But we wave and cry happily.

Photi does not wave. He stands stiffly at the helm. He wears his bank guard's cap and Champoiseau's costume. We see his powdered gray hair, his wrinkled skin. He seems a bad likeness of himself. He seems in danger of petrifying as this bad likeness of himself.

We see a lump on his forehead.

Cameras zoom in on him. He remains stiffly upright, as if tied to a mast. The lenses feast on his face, the tear-tipped sorrow of his eyes.

The clipper is tied up, but Photi does not move. He stands on deck, in profile with the shrouded statue, a shared silhouette.

We crowd close. Hushed and motionless, we await his words. He stares at us, and when his black-shadowed eyes finally move, they are like those of a goat, a goat that is about to leap and run out of reach.

Susanna glares at him.

"*Adelphia mou,*" he finally says, and stops.

Pindaros arrives at the dock. He, too, stands hushed and motionless.

Photi sees his father. "*Patera mou,*" he says, and stops. "Susanna," he says, and stops.

Then softly, to our anxious assembly, he begins. "We were wayfarers together, you and I." He pauses. He can say nothing more. He raises his hand. Trembling, his hand reaches the shroud. He pulls it away.

We blink. We stare. The statue seems a bad likeness of herself.

O God in heaven! We grab our foreheads. Have we not seen this Nike before? Have we — O God in heaven! — not seen this Nike before?

We stand stupefied. The sound of Susanna's cameras grind exceedingly fine and loud.

Our hands stop our eyes from seeing. We moan. We groan. We cry.

PART FOUR

❧ 1 ❧

*T*HE PAIN IS NEVER OLD.

Today, in our homes, when we play Susanna's video again and hear again the words Photi found voice to utter to us that black morning, we cry anew.

Anew we follow him into the sanctuary. Anew he sits on an ancient rock. Anew we listen.

We call it the apologia.

The video never tires. It whirs on like tackle yarn, a sorrow to itself.

No, it is not to pay a penance that we press Play, nor is it to expiate or exculpate. We play the video because it is one of the keenest yet saddest joys of the spirit to watch a man plunge headlong from a height he chose to climb. We play it because, as in Aeschylus and Sophocles, we feel an exalted calm, the calm that comes when you can only say at the end: what happened had to happen.

In truth, you see, it is only now and then that we play the video, just as now and then we will go to watch in a theater a Prometheus, an Oedipus. Just as now and then we will take up a book of astronomy, hold it a moment to feel its weight, and then open it anywhere to learn a little about the stars.

❧ 2 ❧

THE APOLOGIA OF PHOTI ANTHROPOTIS:

Adelphia mou, the sky is on my head. Hollow the earth, it could not contain my sorrow.

Susanna, let roll your cameras. I am Photi Anthropotis, your finale.

The Louvre has our Nike, and I am but this tale of sorrow for you to document, to sell.

Adelphia mou, you saw me as Champoiseau in a wheelchair, saw me hop the prow and climb the wings. I do not fly
off to heaven. I come down. Gabrielle does not recognize
me, costumed and aged as I am. I sit in the wheelchair. She
stands beside me.

The piano movers bring the plank for the 1939 scene.

I sneeze. The ceremonial flowers! I sneeze again. I
itch. The makeup. I perspire. I am embarrassed. I need water. Would the guard please bring an ancient actor a glass of
water? She goes to bring me one.

The plank is down. The piano movers lead our shrouded
Nike down the stairs.

Gabrielle returns with the water. My wheelchair is
empty.

Adelphia mou, you saw the old French army van, saw our
Nike loaded into it like a horse. You saw me in the passenger seat. I sat there praying to God . . . and down the boule-
vard races a man on a bicycle. The actor Champoiseau! You
wish you could not remember him. He leaps off his bike
and dashes into the Louvre. He shouts to Gabrielle, "The
real Nike? Is this the real Nike?"

Gabrielle looks at the Nike on the prow. The fake! Terror. Gone, the Nike gone! She runs down the stairs, through

the Hall of Antiquities, out the door. She looks into the van. "Photi!" she shrieks with amazement. "Photi!" she exclaims with delight. "Are you crazy?"

The rear door is swung closed. Gabrielle opens the driver's door and pounces into the seat. Susanna's propman/driver is trying to secure the rear door. Off she goes, tires complaining, into night streets of Paris. I toss away the medal.

Gabrielle is a driving daredevil. She gives her cap an off-duty tilt. She smiles at me. "D'Artagnan," she says, and squeezes my hand affectionately.

She veers around a corner. A couple in love is crossing the street. She halts suddenly. The couple passes. She speeds on.

I listen for police sirens. What I hear is a groan. Our Nike groaning? I look back. Incredible! It is Champoiseau, lying in the cargo space at the feet of our shrouded Nike. He is exhausted, breathing in gulps.

"Who is that?" asks Gabrielle.

Champoiseau, I reply, an *acteur*. The original.

He pursued us on his bike. When Gabrielle stopped for the couple to cross, he leaped into the van through the windowed rear door, which the driver had no chance to lock.

Champoiseau groans. A heart attack? I reach back and feel the pulse in his neck. I tell Gabrielle we must leave him at a hospital.

"No," protests the *acteur*, and swallows a glycerine tablet.

He reaches up and touches my shoulder in an imploring way. "I stay, Kyrie Photi. I am on a mission."

Mission? I ask.

"Repatriation." His breathing slows. He grins and looks up at our Nike.

Devilishly he pulls down the shroud. "Eureka!" he proclaims, and gives his little titter laugh. He recites: "'O! that this too too solid flesh would melt, thaw and resolve itself into a dew.'"

I do not like his emoting. I do not like his pulling down the shroud without asking.

Though it pleases me that he is beneath the notice of our Nike, and that his head occupies the space reserved for the round end of a horse, I worry that he might die.

He and I are mannequins — I, a Champoiseau in nineteenth-century French finery and gold cufflinks; he, a Champoiseau in the jersey and leggings of a cyclist.

"Doppelgänger," he says to me. "Who is whose?"

I do not like his question. He has too much breath now.

He critiques our Nike: "Not in the grand style of the Phidian age. Sculptor unknown. Decorative figure, of late period. The Aegean doll of immature intellects. But any way you slice her, a survivor."

His eyes sleepily close. "*Bon soir*, Mademoiselle Fifi," he says to the statue, and he rests his head against the back of my seat to snooze.

I say a silent prayer. Though I pray for him, I confess that I resent his nearness to the toes of our Nike, and as he drowses, I resent the peace that communion with her spirit seems to have bestowed on his face.

My sisters and brothers, how it thrills me to be so close to our Nike! Even with this disagreeable actor at her feet, even seen in the dim cargo space of a 1939 French cavalry van, our Nike is a glory. But now that I have her, I feel the terror of losing her.

We reach the open road of the countryside. I turn on the radio.

French night radio, blandly musical, interrupted by no bulletin of news. Paris sleeps. The world, without its Victory, spins ever on.

Gabrielle smiles at me, an excited smile. She seems glad that things will never be the same for her.

The night is deep. The van smells like a haybarn, yet I feel trapped as if in a theater.

Yes, I have our Nike, but I have brought a ghost. The *acteur*. He stirs and sits up now, lotus position. His shoulders bump against the back of my seat. He breathes easily. When he speaks he is onstage, a droning Greek chorus, except that he is French and a gadfly.

He addresses the night and Gabrielle and me: "Two Nikes, two Champoiseaus, two repatriators. Two guards." He titters and pokes his finger at me. "You on your island with its shallow creed — I back here in this aromatic univan universe with nothing but horse hairs to sit on and museumdom's *piece de résistance* breathing down on me from her throatless neck."

He laughs at his predicament — his audience sitting with its back to him. He moans, "Only Greek gods do this to an *acteur*," and admonishes himself, "In reduced circumstances, one must show savoir-faire, elegance of spirit."

"Kyrie Photi," he says, "your goddess is headless for a purpose: so she cannot witness our petty, laughable world, our posings, our travails, our pitiful defeats."

I frown. I know he calls me Kyrie Photi to mock Susanna. He moves forward a little and his head, face up, pops into the gearbox space between Gabrielle and me. He is like an annoying sleeve puppet.

"Look at you," he says to me, "you impostor! My vest, my shoes, my gold cufflinks. Hair powdered gray, face wrinkled, they even gave you crow's-feet eyes. Guard of the cherished findspot! Ha! Find yourself, Kyrie Photi, forget the spot."

His puppet face pops up at Gabrielle. "Stop the van, *ma garde!* Stop this highway robbery. You are French. Where can you go with a Greek statue?"

Gabrielle is silent.

"Phone *le musée,*" he orders her.

Her response is increased speed. Down and up the hills of wine country.

He repeats, "Where *can* you go with a Greek statue?"

I believe the air of the vineyards is making him tipsy.

The actor quiets, sits back, his eyes close. He slumps. I reach behind and feel his neck for pulse. "I am well, Kyrie Photi," he tells me. "*Acteurs* die in the *third* act."

He sleeps.

Total darkness. Soon the Alps, Italy. We speed on, through a forest, our headlights a torrent. Gabrielle and I share a loaf of bread, and I sip wine from a bottle. On the radio I find the songs of Aznavour. Gabrielle gives me glances, affectionate glances.

The lyrics say there is love, there is passion, but does destiny leave me time?

I touch Gabrielle's hand on the wheel. So much I owe her. So much do I owe Susanna.

Aznavour sings on. In the mountains, our van labors in the thinning air.

Champoiseau wakes, sits up in the lotus position.

I pass bread and wine back to him.

He gulps from the bottle. "No night for songs," he tells Gabrielle. "Turn down the radio. This is a night for reckoning."

She turns down the radio.

With a flourish, he announces, "The cast:

"Gabrielle: Bonnie.

"Photi Anthropotis: Clyde.

"Champoiseau: hero repatriator.

"*La Victoire:* goddess in distress.

"Theme: love does not conquer all.

"No applause. No intermission."

"Written and directed by, and manipulated by, Mother of Sorrows — Susanna. For the worst of reasons."

He addresses Gabrielle. "Keeper of the guard," he warns, "you will pay the piper. You will be vilified in France, hunted down, extradited, convicted, sent to jail — traitors' jail, where the guards twist necks and crack bones."

Gabrielle gives him the Victory sign with one finger.

I turn to the actor and ask, "Frenchman, what is *your* game?"

He likes the cue. "My game? *Acteur,*" he announces. "Jumping into this van to stop your diabolical escape — all act. Less patriotic than slightly unhinged. The script is in my head. Always a role — that is me, my life — amusingly godless one day, as Tartuffe; marvelously mesmerizing the next, as Hippolyte in *Phèdre.* Today, a foiler, if not foil myself. Ha! I am Champoiseau, though you wear my cufflinks. I heroize classicism, shovel dirt for it. But in you, Kyrie Photi, I have found my *frère* peanut shell. We are kings back to back, kings of infinite space."

His hand knocks on the roof of the van. Infinite space. The sound, he pretends, terrifies him. "Chasms outside," he warns. "The night is deep. Immensities without. We are the last of humanity, rolling in this bumpy caisson."

Gabrielle is agitated. She turns up the radio.

"Forget Aznavour," he says. "He will sing you into submission."

She turns the volume higher.

I rub Gabrielle's neck to soothe her. I warm her hands on the wheel. There is so little reference to the archangels in Scripture, I say to myself, but Gabrielle seems to me like one.

Champoiseau is quiet. He could flee from the rear door and have the police chase us, shoot our tires, pounce with their nightsticks on us.

Why are you here? I ask.

He laughs. "Pass up performance in a van? Pass up worldwide approval? The grand prix passion play? Who needs a theater, a proscenium arch?"

I ask him, What were Susanna's worst of reasons?

"Emasculation," he replies. "Off with the epaulets. Vagina dentata. The toothy, monstrous fairy godmother."

This attractive woman a toothy monster, a Gorgona?

"In person," he says. "Each male she celebrates, she denigrates. She robs him of his stones. Clip clip. Michelangelo's weakness for glorified maleness, El Greco's for pandering to the grandees while he snorted the fires of the Inquisition. 'Silhouette of Victory.' Ha! Bah! Better, 'Silhouette of Manipulation.' Her banjo, Photi Anthropotis, Exhibit One."

I ask myself: I, Exhibit One? I, her banjo? The wine talks.

On mocks Champoiseau: "Ascension, Mother wants? The grandest theme of humankind? Ha! Bah! For every male a failing, a fall. Silhouettes, she calls her PBS stories. Ha! Bah! On each artwork she leaves a shadow *pathétique*, and that is *her* silhouette."

Why? I ask. How can this be?

"She is Electra. Screwing her dead father by diminishing men — great men, small men, all men."

I ponder.

"Her father loved cheap blondes, not her. He sent her off — far off, campuses, excursions. Willed his fortune to harlots and died in a snowdrift." The *acteur* grunts. "Half the story. This poor little girl lined up a solid row of grown men when she was nineteen, took them on free. This poor little girl hoped Daddy would return by sunset to the top of the hill. But if not, or until then, somebody else's daddy, any older man, would do. Forget her crew. Leitmotif. She puts them in short pants, their rocks tight; they work harder for her that way. She keeps them near, to pay her a kiss when she wants one. No pets allowed. They'd screw her if she said so — the propman first — but she won't. She's off men, all of them. She's a frozen surface. The woman in her has not survived her childhood. *Le grand désillusionnement* of little girls: Daddy as a departed spirit, to be called back and gotten even with. How it does live on and die hard in older girls who wear mauve and, sometimes, no panties."

I reflect on this sadness about older girls.

Bitterly, he says, "Mother can add 'Accomplice in Larceny' to her credits now. She's just another purveyor of stolen treasure."

My face itches. It is the makeup Susanna has painted on me. I open the window for air.

"Anagnorisis," Champoiseau declares, "elusive self-recognition," and his face pops up at me from below. "You, the Greek who accepts no substitutes, you who pines for the genuine mother-goddess and wants to — splash splash — start up her fountain again. Ha! The waters backward do not run. Photi Anthropotis is not rescuing his queen from the dragon on the Seine, he is tossing her purity to the wolves — what is left of it. Oh, the pity! She will become a tiresome TV star, a cheap symbol, no more a work of art than the Mobil Oil red Pegasus. Victory? *La Victoire de Samothrace was* Victory. Now she is the world's 'victim of the hour' and stands among the horse hairs, and I tickle her ankle."

Pas permis, I say sharply. I will not allow his hand on our Nike.

Gabrielle smiles. She has been there.

I scowl. I sit with arms folded, in disgust.

He removes his hand and sits upright. "Kyrie Photi," he says, "you have proved the Louvre penetrable. Now give Mother what she deserves. Her finale *magnifique.* The *faux* Nike coming home! How colossal, hilarious!"

His arm reaches Gabrielle. He nudges her. "Call the Louvre, *ma garde.* Bring the impostor here in a van. She has had her stupefying moment in history. Exchange her, Nike for Nike. Escort this incessant national treasure back in the van. Repatriate her. All France will love you."

Then he delivers this shot: "All France will love you — he will not."

I pray for strength to keep my ire from rising. Do not listen, Gabrielle, I plead. He is demented, he is an actor.

Annoyed, she accelerates.

I fear we will smash with terrible thunder into a huge

boulder or a tree. Found in the ruined van: three bodies and our Nike cracked to pieces.

Champoiseau resumes his concocted libretto: "Already on the TVs of the world, *la Victoire* has top position on the news. They are making her a superstar, a joke — an all-purpose metaphor for *faux* and real — take your pick. Is she or is she not? You will hear her name in the rhetoric of politicians, in the exhortations of priests, the laments of poets. You think she has a pallor? Ha! See her *couleur* deepen now when *artistes* do renditions: no more champagne sorbet. Nike purple now, Nike *bleu*, Nike fuchsia and plum, every mournful durable pigment in the palette."

Halt, I shout, but he continues: "I have seen the crucifix with a detachable Christ. Soon in the shops, statuettes of Gabrielle with detachable wings! Is this the fate Photi Anthropotis desires for his Gabrielle?"

I boil. If I were to speak, I would spit first.

"Poor Gabrielle," he laments, as if already she is in chains. "The payer of the price, the martyr, the Louvre's own Joan."

Gabrielle weeps. She slows down. She feels tired, miserable, cursed.

"Where can you go with a Greek statue?" he singsongs.

She stops the van. We are in deep woods, woods so deep Champoiseau will not walk away. She steps out of the van.

I go and stand with her. We listen to the sounds of birds; we watch the moon, which seems to drift over Italy. She takes my hand. I lift her cap and kiss her.

The actor spies us from the rear window. He smiles.

She kisses me, kisses me as if my kiss were true but not true enough.

Champoiseau opens the rear door and steps down from the van. "Have I permission to escape?" he asks. "You have mine."

He selects a tree to sleep under. He lies down, a proscenium of branches over his head. We can leave him, drive off. How does he know we will not? Driving off is not in his script. We are *his*, in *his* script — the puppet is now our puppeteer.

I give him a horse blanket. He smiles. *"Merci,"* he says gratefully.

I take off my costume. Gabrielle removes her uniform. We enter the rear of the van. Beneath the presence of our Nike, we cover ourselves with the shroud to fall asleep in each other's arms.

We hear Champoiseau chortle. "End, Act One," he announces to the night.

❦ 3 ❦

THE NEXT MORNING, we dust off the horse hairs and are rolling again through the breezy Alps. I turn on the radio. Still no Louvre in the news.

Sitting on the floor, his back against my seat again, the actor drinks wine. His tune starts again. "The sculptor of this stone would laugh. Your love is such a doomed little tale of venery."

"I love Photi," protests Gabrielle. "Would I be driving this van if I did not?"

"You are a desperate woman," Champoiseau chides, "who believes Victory has been invented to find you a man. The angels of the Lord have not brought you a man, but *la Victoire de Samothrace* has. What a simple fool you are, Gabrielle. Stop the van. Phone the Louvre. Make a deal.

They bring the dummy to the dock, your Greek goes home with it to his findspot and his bicycle, and you end this high-flying misbehavior and bring Mademoiselle Fifi to Paris."

"No," says Gabrielle. "The Nike is theirs before she is ours. Paris is tired of her eerie fidelity. I am tired of her eerie fidelity."

The actor laughs. "What a noble *garde*. You would part with the *Mona Lisa* if the right Italian came along."

I console Gabrielle, kiss her. Her hand comes to rest on my thigh.

We wind through mountain passes. On the radio a woman yodels, sings of heights. Our tires sing too; they have long outrun their zest for highways.

Still no news, no police.

Soon Milan. And Vérité a long coastline away. I wish for an armful of laurel to give this van fragrance.

Champoiseau drowsily peers up at the Nike and winks at her. "I would trade you for a fruit stand," he says, then slumbers once more.

Gabrielle turns off the radio. She is with her thoughts, I with mine. How lucky I am, I say to myself. Our Nike in cargo and Gabrielle at the wheel. I soothe her neck and warm her driving hands. Her thoughts do not comfort her. She says nothing. She slows, then speeds up.

Milan. Soon the coast and down the leg of Italy. The Adriatic. Soon Vérité. Soon the clipper . . . the Aegean. *Thalatta! Thalatta!* The arrival, the jubilation. The fi-na-le!

Soon darkness. Champoiseau sleeps.

Gabrielle is glum. She slows. "A figurine with detachable wings?" she says to me. The thought has dismayed her.

Taunts, I say. Forget his taunts.

She pulls off the road and stops in front of a roadside trattoria. It is closed.

She is weeping. She looks back at our Nike. "Why can I not see myself without her?" she asks. "Was it for her I commandeered this van, or for you?"

I feel distressed. She looks at me and I offer her my silk Champoiseau handkerchief. She does not accept it. I bring my shoulder close for her to rest on. She does not want my shoulder.

"To what purpose these roads?" she asks. "To be with her . . . or with you . . . in your kitchen with a sink for an altar?"

I have no answer.

"Everything has been made fraudulent," she says, "and yet you, I feel, are the noblest of men."

I take her hands and caress them. I say to her, Ah, you are petite and lovely, Gabrielle. Our island will shower its gratitude on you. It will go bonkers. I touch her nose. Ab-so-lute-ly.

"Pas permis," says the guard in her. We do not laugh.

With the silk handkerchief I wipe her tears.

She tells me, "Pascal says that the heart has its reasons of which reason knows nothing."

I want to think about Pascal's homily, but the right rear tire is deflating.

Gabrielle opens the door and listens to the tire go down.

I follow her out. How do you fix a flat? I ask.

She, too, is puzzled.

Champoiseau climbs out of the rear door with a tire iron and a jack. He could run off, call the police, the French army. He could attack us with the iron. And indeed, he theatrically swings it to limber up his arms. He looks at us pitifully. Two hits and the Nike is his. All Paris is his.

He moves toward us.

Gabrielle cringes. I raise my arm to shield her from the blow.

"I crave blood," he histrionically terrorizes, and swings the iron wildly. "I hate marble." He seethes with anger and turns to look at the van. The Nike? Double murder is more to his taste. He pivots back to us and swings again. The iron hits and adheres to an imaginary wall. He tries mightily to pull the iron from the wall, but it will not budge. He is foiled. He gives up. The Fates have spared his victims.

"Yours is a love made in heaven," Champoiseau declares. "Who can kill you?"

His little show over, he laughs. He puts the tire iron down, rolls up his sleeves, and squats by the wheel. Off comes the tire and on goes the spare. His hands are soiled. He comes to me and removes the silk Champoiseau handkerchief from my vest. He wipes his hands on it, stuffs it back.

"Cinderella." He bows. "Your coach awaits."

He enters the rear of the van and resumes the slumber position.

Gabrielle looks at me. She does not want to get back into the van.

"I must call," she says.

The Louvre?

Her lips quiver. *"Oui."*

I implore her, No. No.

"Forgive me," she says. "I love you." Tears begin again.

I do not understand, I say. You are listening to this lunatic?

Softly, she says, "Where can you go with a Greek statue?"

She walks toward the trattoria, to an outside phone booth.

I look away. I cannot bear to watch my destiny dialed out in a dumb phone booth. I listen to the evening sounds of Italy. Birds singing as if they have no way out of the sky, cars speeding as if they have heard on the radio that the Nike of Samothrace has been stolen and thus there will be no tomorrow. Tomorrow?

Adelphia mou, I think of you and your promised tomorrow. No joy to uncork, no euphoria. Nothing to say to me. No reason ever to look at me again. Foiled by an *acteur.* I would commandeer the wheel and roar down this road — if I knew gearshifts. I would rope myself like a haversack to the back of her — if our Nike could fly.

"She will be back," says Champoiseau. "She has a well of desolation for a heart. She will not phone."

I want to believe him.

"Angel Gabrielle will be yours to keep," he prophesies. "You are her treasure. But *caveat emptor: les femmes* French are never soothingly phlegmatic."

His face pops up from the gearbox. "*Mon ami,* she will

guard you like a treasure." He sits back and takes a gulp from the wine bottle. He has seen enough of my face, and I of his.

"Look at you," he says. "You sit with the forward-bent pose of the chariot driver, in *my* costume, *my* makeup. I think you are a stooge, Kyrie Photi. You seek the forever redeeming female. The Nike. Ha! Bah! She is your wound *splendide*. Without your wound, what would you be? Who would listen to your bike bell?"

I say nothing. Dignity dictates that I say nothing.

The actor laughs. "And, ah yes, your round bedside marble. The maternal breast. It is hardly a hominid fragment two million years old. Toss it. Roll it off a cliff. Wean thyself, Kyrie Photi. You have the Nike now, the whole whore."

I lunge back at him. I am a human windmill of fists, feet, and elbows.

He drops the wine bottle at his feet. I have his throat in my hands. I squeeze. The statue moves, teeters. I do not stop squeezing. From teetering to tilting to toppling, down she will go.

To save her, I release the neck of Champoiseau, but I trip over the bottle and collapse. Our Nike falls toward me.

Her hem strikes my head. For a moment she is like a beast. My arms brace mightily to ease her weight . . . and save my family nose, my body, my life.

I shut my eyes and hold my breath. She has fallen on me and I am not dead. I have saved her! I breathe again. Our Nike — glory to God! — is whole, each contour, each plume intact.

Gabrielle returns and finds me compressed under the marble. My eyes are closed. She is frantic. "Do you breathe?" she cries. "Are you alive?"

I half open my eyes.

Gabrielle's head is above me, enwinged between the wings, as if she will sing me a hurdy-gurdy song. She lowers her face and kisses me.

My eyes open wide. I draw a Christian breath. I am euphoric in this miraculous condition, and yet I say to myself, O come quick, Death, come! Never have I been so ready as now.

Gabrielle kneels and wedges her shoulders under the wings of the Nike. She lifts. She lifts. I feel it is unnecessary of her to insist so much that I live. Let me die, I want to say, but I push and push.

Champoiseau sits up and rubs his neck, soothing where

he swallowed his words. He looks at my leveraged predicament, and he too wedges his shoulder under the wings. He grunts. He lifts. Gabrielle lifts.

Three together, agonizing, we ease our great marble marvel upward, away from my flattened heap of bones.

Rocking a little, our Nike comes to her feet. Resurrected once more!

Gabrielle and I embrace, slump to the floor.

She feels the lump on my forehead. "*Mon chéri!*" she exclaims, and kisses my lump. "Your Nike is telling us something."

Gabrielle, I say, *you* are telling me something.

The showman applauds our declarations.

I leave the van. A toe is broken. I limp. I sit on a rock under a tree. Gabrielle comes and sits with me.

With dread I ask her, The Louvre?

"No," she says, "no."

I embrace her. I kiss her.

Tearfully she says, "If I call, my heart would stop."

Champoiseau watches us from the rear door. He pretends to take aim and hurl a dart at us. With a sad chortle he proclaims, "Act Three."

D<small>AYBREAK</small>. Down the Adriatic coast we roll. The police car behind us has no reason to stop us and ask, Where are you taking this horse?

Back to back we sit, Champoiseau and Champoiseau. He sips at the wine left in the bottle. "Esprit de corps," he explains, and then his singsong starts: "Where *can* you go with a Greek statue? Clear the ground for new creations."

I am sick of him. I need a drink. Mind reading, he offers the bottle, the final sip. I wipe the neck on my sleeve.

I feel a strange sadness, a shamefulness. I cannot believe that I had the hands and the heart and the strength to choke Champoiseau. I, Photi Anthropotis, a strangler? Over a statue. Over a callous comment.

I think of my father, how much he endured from me, how much he wanted a noble son to wear his cap and carry his name. A murderer for a son! Oh, would my father cry out: What have I, Pindaros Anthropotis, done to pique the Furies?

Champoiseau broods. That, too, is an act.

My fingers feel the blessed lump on my head; it is not as large as I would like. I look at Gabrielle, who is not as petite as I would want her to believe she is; has ever a woman done for a man what she is doing for me? How lucky I am, I say to myself, to have a lump from our Nike to touch and a kiss from Gabrielle to remember.

I think of our new life on Samothrace. Gabrielle and I, both in uniform, standing guard. She with her cap set just so, and I with mine. The streamlets giggling again, our Nike momentous again, her feet touching down again on her fountain stones. Passing boats tooting three dots and a dash, three dots and a dash. Tooting our Nike. Tooting us — two guards in love.

I see Gabrielle on a bicycle. She is beautiful and not unhappy, and I am on a bicycle too, and we pedal for the summit of Fengari. I wave to the women of our villages. No more do they seek to do little favors for me. They see Gabrielle and smile suffering smiles among themselves; they seem to have had poorly digested dinners. And the men no longer give me tcheek-tcheek; they thank the Lord I have a wife now, finally! They do their crosses when they see me. No daughters need worry them now.

I name the flowers I would bring to Gabrielle if I were not allergic: asters and asphodels, violets and zinnias. And in my mind I see her snow-white cat, and I am happy the cat is not in Paris, hungry atop the abandoned bed of Gabrielle. I see the cat take its length up the wall to my roof, and it occupies my slingchair, and I am glad to have a slingchair for this cat to occupy. And my father in America — I think of him and ask myself, Would anything I do make him happy? And yet I feel if he came back to our island, all would be right. He would love Gabrielle and, through her, love me, and he would call me pebblehead no longer and we would be a family. And my mother — of her, too, I think. I remember her large eyes, hazel ones like Gabrielle's, how fierce my mother's eyes grew when she turned them on me and warned me, "I have my stick." Such love my mother had for me. Never did she let my faults go unremarked upon or uncorrected, never did she hobble me with sympathy.

O Mother, I lament, one child you had, and it had to be me.

Truly, she would love Gabrielle, whose righteous stature

and eyes and noble heart are like hers, and whose kisses are as sweet.

I touch Gabrielle's buttons. Her fingers come to mine to give them encouragement.

I breathe in the Adriatic. Will the seas cease to be eternal? I ask, and Gabrielle answers, "Where would the goldfish swim?"

"Where *can* you go with a Greek statue?" singsongs the actor. "Clear the ground for new creations."

Sleep, I say with irritation, and the self-mesmerized actor slumps sideways and sleeps.

Think of the findspot as an omphalos, say the French. I do, my sisters and brothers, I think of it that way — a navelmark — and think how strange that you and I and everyone have a navelmark, and our Nike too has a navelmark, and what was this unknown sculptor thinking? That she was born of a mother? not born of our dreams? That, too, I will think about when I am home and my bird feeder is full and my nightlight is on and I look out at the cold heights of Fengari.

Vérité, nine miles away. My heart speeds up. Is there a Vérité? Is there a clipper waiting? I think of snowdrifts and Cadillacs and El Greco and the dead grandee. Too much would be rubbed away, I said to Susanna, but she buried my marble anyway. Her documentary will start a style, win awards, she said. She did not say a wrong will be righted, did not say justice will be done. She said, win awards. Have awards evolved over the thousands of years of small human struggles, or have poetry and art and sculpture? Yes, she and I have something to prove, she to her father, I to mine — and to ourselves. Are we moths to the same flame, ascension? Or smoke of the same flame, ascension? Up, up — to what? I itch under Susanna's makeup and creams. The harsh, brash words of this actor cause me irritation, and I may have to curse.

I look at Gabrielle and ask myself, If mountains came out of the sea, did seabirds too? And I think how gulls fly with wings that are broken, even at night they fly. In an entirely different world, I say to myself, wings would not break, there would be lands and oceans in which birds never fell, and there would be no real, no fake, no great, no small, no Phidias, no Photi. No Photi to kneel to Susanna, and be stooge to her.

We pass a Mobil station with its red Pegasus. No, never was there a Perseus or a Bellerophon or a fountain on Mount Helicon, and all the liver-eating eagles and the fiery-

tongued serpents, these too there were not. But there *is* a
Photi Anthropotis, I say, and my name is not one to hide
under a cap — it is mine, like the ring around the moon is
the moon's.

In all the universe, nothing so resembles God as the human soul, and I ask myself, If Photi Anthropotis is a soul
and resembles God, is he not then a light, a *phos*, a Photi,
however dim or bright or pathetic?

I perspire. I ask myself too many questions. My heart is
saying this way, this way, and my mind is saying that way,
that way. And this antiquated cavalry van with singing tires
seems like a proud edifice now, not a haybarn, and inside it
I lift my shoulders and say to myself, Photi, you are not a
lunatic knight, you are not a stooge.

Off beyond an overpass, a taverna.

Stop, I say to Gabrielle.

She drives to the taverna grounds and parks near a fig
tree. I turn to her, take hold of her hands, and tell her I feel
we are an off-key marching band. I tell her my mind is racing with thoughts and I feel the day is never new. Always it
is an old one coming back. I tell her this is a sensation I have
had since infancy — an old day coming back. I tell her
about my life. Defeat and sorrow, allergies, nets that are

sieves, poems that are unpublishable. I tell her about my father, who stole my bride as Champoiseau stole our Nike. I tell her about my caïque swallowed by the sea and my whaler's hat that floated one rebellious minute, then sank like a crust of bread.

She stares. I look away from her eyes, but there is nothing outside to see when I look away. My eyes go back to her, her stare. A part of me is Champoiseau, I say, the real Champoiseau. What he felt, I felt. I rolled through his dying day in a wheelchair, in his clothes, and felt his glory, his reunion, his farewell. I rose up as he rose up. I felt the pride he felt. His spirit gave my legs springs to hop the prow, to gain the wings. His spirit commanded, Climb, Photi Anthropotis, climb. I climbed. I ascended! I felt the awe of the sky void of earth. I saw the mirror of almighty God, which is the glory and the sense of all the universe, and then, *ma chérie*, I felt peace, a shimmering peace, like a bright golden sea when there is no wind.

Gabrielle's stare persists. She keeps her hands in mine.

My heart is thumping, I say to her. I feel an inexpressible dread. I tell her: A folk wisdom says, We ride for the fall we take. But you, my pretty one, I cannot let fall.

I look back at our Nike. O beautiful dream, I say to her,

you are like an ambushed bird, and I must make a prudent raising of a window and let you go.

I turn to Gabrielle. I say, Phone the Louvre.

Her hands pull away from mine. "No," she implores. "No."

A police car passes.

I tell her, I do not love you.

She begins to weep. She shakes her head. She does not believe what I said.

Do I? I ask myself. Do I believe what Photi Anthropotis said? That voice was Photi Anthropotis? Or Champoiseau, the one original Champoiseau? The one no fake French medal pinned.

Gabrielle has looked away from me. Tears have wet her nose. I say to her: You deserve happiness, a prince. Quiet departure by coach.

Accept no substitutes, I say to her.

I plead with her: Phone *le musée*. Tell them. They must come to Vérité. Nike for Nike. Go back to Paris with this "incessant national treasure." You will be celebrated. Tell them how you turned the tables on the poor *excentrique* named Photi Anthropotis. They will eulogize you as they eulogized Champoiseau. An orchestra will play "La Marseillaise."

She does not move.

Go, I demand, or I will do it myself.

She removes her cap. She opens the door and steps out. She places her cap on the seat. Weeping, she walks toward the taverna.

I hold my fingers still and do not touch her cap.

I watch Gabrielle enter the taverna.

I turn to Champoiseau. He is not there.

I look down the road, up the road. I do not see him. I see a roadside fruit stand. I run to it. I see customers, peaches, pears, melons. No Champoiseau.

Has he wings, a disguise? Is he a kumquat plant, a mango? I limp back to the van and stand under the fig tree. I am puzzled. I hate his disappearance. It is another stunt, I say to myself. He has shrunk himself and is hiding in the gearbox. He has commandeered a bike.

The sun strikes through the branches.

I feel he is watching me, happy as a dog with two tails.

I hear a rustle above me. I look up. He is there in the branches. The hypotenuse of a right triangle. Chewing on a fig.

"Fig?" he offers, and reaches to pluck one.

He reaches too far. Arms up, like a chutist, he plummets. His body hits the top of the van with a terrible thunder. He lies spread-eagled.

I am aghast.

He stirs. His breath short, his eyes dazed.

Heart seizure? I climb to the top. He lifts his hand to show me something.

A fig.

"Tree-ripened," he says to me.

I tell him I will call an ambulance.

He stops me. "No, *mon ami*. I am like a man who has taken the poison cup."

His head rises and he looks toward the sky. "Look up," he says.

I look up. At the tree.

"The sky," he demands. "Sky! Sky!" He says the word as if he has lived through three acts of his life just to vocalize that word.

I look to the sky.

"We are gulls, Kyrie Photi," he says. "But the sky shits on us."

He grins. His knuckles form a fist. He performs three quick knocks on top of the van, then, in tempo, a heavy one. Beethoven's fate-knocking Fifth.

Cars and trucks streak by on the highway.

I grasp his shoulders to help him rise. I hold him tightly as we climb down from the roof together, arms intertwined, bodies embracing. We struggle forward to the rear door. I slide it open.

He lies down on his back, his head at the feet of our Nike. He is cargo again. He looks up at her and says to me, "Banjo, keep her. She is yours . . ."

He grasps my hand, breathes three quick breaths, then a deeply sighing long one. His last.

I remove his hand from mine, then press my ear to his chest.

No heartbeat. I thrust my mouth on his mouth to fill him with my breath. I pump his chest. I try and try to give him breath.

I fail.

I cross myself. I sign a cross over him. I ask God to have mercy on his soul. I cover him with a horse blanket, although this actor does not seem averse to pleasing the flies.

The shadow of Nike falls on the blanket. The shadow is sloped like a mountain.

I feel a heavy sorrow. I feel I am inside a haybarn after the horse has been taken from it, and the horse, being there no longer, becomes a phantom, just fallen hair, a blanket, an odor, and nothing else.

Death ends a life, I say to myself; it does not end a companionship.

I close the rear door and walk with a limp over to a tree closer to the taverna. I sit under it. I hear birds: Tcheek-tcheek.

Gabrielle leaves the taverna and is walking toward me. Her eyes are wet. She carries a loaf of bread.

She twists the bread into pieces and scatters them. I look at the crusts. I say to myself: A bird for each crust. Somewhere, for each bird there is a crust.

I look into Gabrielle's eyes and ask, They will come?

She nods.

I embrace her.

We enter the van. I say to myself, Forward, lamefoot! Forward to Vérité.

She starts the engine. She asks, "Sometime, will you come to Paris?"

No, I answer.

"I will come to you," she says.

⤛ *5* ⤜

PHOTI'S APOLOGIA ENDS. He walks away, beyond the dock, past the hotel, the acacia trees. He seems to have shed everything except his French clothes, and wants to empty his island of himself.

TV news crews clamber off the next boat. We are like a house filling with callers. They expect to see jubilation, Dionysian revelry. Instead, we look pummeled. Even our magnolias, which sulk.

Where is the Victory man? they ask.

He has gone for a walk, we say. And he did, limping a little in his fancy-toed consul shoes. No suitcase — the purple-blue one was abandoned in Paris. Where did he go? they ask. He went to his house.

And, verily, he did. We tell them no more.

We do not tell them he stopped at his door to look into the bird feeder. Empty. He knocked on the door.

No one opened it. He went to the kitchen window. He saw his father sitting inside, glaring at the obsolete calendar. In the sink he had dumped the marble fragment. When he saw Photi at the window, he rose from the chair, but not to open the door. He rose to turn on the faucet, then he sat and watched the gushing water purify the marble.

Photi limped away toward Mount Fengari. We saw him reach the trail that leads to the summit. As if his bike, too, had forsaken him, he trudged upward, alone.

～ 6 ～

WE SEE THE TWO-A-DAY BOAT ARRIVE. Gabrielle is on it. Out of her uniform, she is smaller than she appeared to us on the video. She is in a meadow-green frock with a white ribbon in her hair. She is pretty, in an Ariadne way. She scans our somber faces.

When she steps from the boat, she carries Photi's

suitcase. She asks for Monsieur Photi Anthropotis. We do not answer. She asks for Susanna.

We point to the hotel. Our fingers are blades. She walks toward the entrance.

Out comes Susanna Regas, in black toreador pants, the strap of her mauve handbag looped through her epaulet. Dark glasses conceal her eyes. She is solemn. In a classical-style painting she would be Hamartia, with a straight nose and unshaded eyes, eyes of holy cruelty.

Her crew has gone. She resides at the hotel to write her next script for PBS. The script elucidates the theme of the middle panel of *The Garden of Earthly Delights*, which some believe shows a dissolute cosmos before the Flood. Others believe it shows the millennium, in which humankind attains a sort of perfection. In this perfect world there are pleasures only, no sins, no cares, and people swarm in the nude and all look alike. There is no ascension in this garden. It seems banished from the cosmos entirely. This melancholic vision demoralized Hieronymus Bosch and caused him, as he completed the panel, a breakdown. He spat on his palette and shouted, "Enough, Mama! Enough!"

Susanna's script will be titled "Silhouette of a Garden." It will, she has told us, even surpass "Repatriation."

She walks over to Gabrielle and leads her to the taverna.

Inside, a photograph of Photi hangs on the wall. It is draped. Taken at sea, the photograph shows Photi in his whaler's cap, aboard his caïque. He reads a book, a Kazantzakis.

Gabrielle weeps.

We watch Susanna. Solemn, unmourning. She does not embrace Gabrielle.

Gabrielle is given a glass of water. She stares at the water but cannot swallow it.

Susanna and Gabrielle leave the taverna. Gabrielle places the purple-blue suitcase under the acacia tree where Photi's bike remains parked. "It is the bike of Kyrie Photi," says Susanna. "He went nowhere without it until he went everywhere without it."

Gabrielle touches the handlebars. She is still weeping.

Susanna leads her to the Sanctuary of the Great Gods.

As if walking to the sad song of a flute, they move slowly through the ancient stones. When they reach the shore, they stand on the pebbly sand and breathe the tender, terrible air. They watch the gentle waves, the cruising gulls.

"It was a Wednesday," says Susanna softly. "Kyrie Photi could not bear another Thursday."

Gabrielle watches Susanna, who seems to be gathering her strength before continuing.

"Still wearing the costume of Champoiseau, with his bank guard's cap, Kyrie Photi descended during the night from Mount Fengari. He walked home. From his vest pockets he supplied the bird feeder with grain and berries he had gathered on the mountain. He knocked on the door. His father opened it.

"They did not speak. Kyrie Photi went into the kitchen. He took the marble fragment from the sink and dried it off with Champoiseau's silk handkerchief. He put it by his bed and placed his mother's wedding wreath on it. He went back to the kitchen. On the obsolete calendar, in the small squares that were not numbered days of December but were empty sky-white spaces, he composed a poem.

"Then he came to my room. He was sobbing uncontrollably. I was just out of the shower. In my robe. I hugged him. Kyrie Photi, I said, you are not wretched. You are not a stooge. You are just one sorry skin in the garden of Hieronymus Bosch. That is what *you* are . . . *we* are. He took off his cap and knelt in front of me. I stood there for him. He opened me. I had just powdered. He was not new to me there. Still sobbing, he inhaled me. I thought he would begin on me, his tongue like a little ice cream spoon. But he didn't. He nicked me, nicked me viciously. I screeched. I smacked his face. He didn't feel it. He was too beaten to feel anything. He put on his cap and walked to the sanctuary, and here, on this ancient sand, he removed his cap, turned it upside down, and filled it with pebbles."

Gabrielle looks out to sea. The waves are like wrists.

"He waded out," says Susanna, "as if he had seen his whaler's hat. He did not wade back. No longer did he fill an observable space. Kyrie Photi is gone."

Gabrielle clasps her mouth in grief.

"A proud swan. A simple duck," says Susanna. "Not flotsam, not jetsam." She awkwardly embraces Gabrielle and says, "How difficult it is to imagine what our lives would be like without the illumination of the lives and deaths, the victories and losses of others."

The embrace ends. Susanna says ruefully, "Kyrie Photi was my fi-na-le. My unfilmed fi-na-le." She opens her handbag. "This was the last prop in my documentary." She extracts Photi's cap and places it on her upraised hand. Stirred by a breeze, the cap for a moment is an effigy.

She offers the cap to Gabrielle. It is accepted.

Susanna extracts the gold cufflinks. She shows these to

Gabrielle but does not part with them. "These, too, were found in the cap." She drops the links back into her bag.

In a mournful, motherly voice Susanna describes the last two minutes of her "Silhouette": "The waves, in close-up, ripple in toward the sand. This sea would give a man burial as in a royal tomb, but these waves do not reach Kyrie Photi's cap and its pebbles. His cap and its pebbles command the screen, while his father, a voice-over, recites the poem Photi wrote on the calendar. There is such human pain in his voice, Photi's father is at one with Kyrie Photi. At one."

She reaches into her bag. A newspaper clipping. It is the poem, bordered in black, untitled, and anonymous.

Solemnly, almost tenderly, she reads the poem to Gabrielle.

> *Adelphia mou*, where
> in this universe we share
> is Nike? Does she fly
> in some oblivion on high?
> Are her wings, a cross
> (a fiction in the sky),
> a cross we see
> our deliverance to be?

> O God the loss, the loss,
> if she is but worth
> one hole in the earth,
> her grave beside the sea.

Sadness holds Susanna silent for a time. Then, as if a screen is about to fade — no, a light of the world is about to fail — she describes the final moment of her "Silhouette": "The waves not reaching the cap of Kyrie Photi have nothing left to do, you see, so the waves and the cap and its pebbles dissolve into whiteness . . . and the credits roll."